# WILD SIDE

*Wilder Irish, book nine*

## MARI CARR

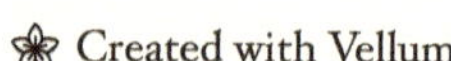 Created with Vellum

*For my family, who feed me, clean up around me, and take it in stride that Mom is probably only half listening when she's at the computer writing.*

# PRAISE FOR WILD SIDE

"One of my favorite **queens of ménage** is at it again!" ★★★★★ *Jennifer, Goodreads*

"Finn is the sweetest, kindness, most loving, **half-witted fool**!" ★★★★★ *Dar, Goodreads*

"Once again Mari Carr has a **hit** on her hands." ★★★★★ *Janet Rodman, Goodreads*

"Mari Carr does it again in this **fantastic addition** to the Collins clan universe." ★★★★★ *Fedora, Goodreads*

"It gets 5 **Flaming hot** stars!!" ★★★★★ *A, Goodreads*

"With a few twists and one scary ass clown they find out that love, **true love has no limits**." ★★★★★ *Sue Andrews, Goodreads*

"**OMG**!!!" ★★★★★ *Xantippi Leska, Goodreads*

"Mari Carr **does it again**!" ★★★★★ *Kitt Crescendo, Goodreads*

# WILD SIDE

*No strings attached? We were wrong. So wrong.*

Layla moved to Baltimore in search of a fresh start. After too many years in a lackluster relationship, she's ready to embrace her wild side. Casual is her new middle name and the last thing she wants or needs is a serious relationship.

Finn and his best friend, Miguel are ALL IN on showing Layla a good time. After all, neither one of them is looking for love either. Or so they think.

Until Finn falls for Layla and Miguel falls for Finn and Layla falls for...both men. Then it's a wild side freefall as the three lovers try to make one plus one plus one equal the perfect match.

PROLOGUE

Patrick Collins peeked in on the baby, checking to make sure Darcy was still sleeping before pulling the door closed and returning to his living room. His four-year-old granddaughter, Sunnie, had finally drifted off on his recliner, spread out like a starfish with one leg resting on the arm of the chair, the other dangling over the raised footrest. Her head was tipped back and her mouth hanging open. He'd turned on *The Lion King* for her and her big brother to watch while he put Darcy down.

Finn was still awake, though barely. His eyes were heavy and he was sucking his thumb, a sure sign he'd be asleep soon. Finn's mother, Riley, was trying to break him of the thumb-sucking habit now that he was in kindergarten and his permanent teeth were starting to come in, but so far she'd had no luck.

Patrick had volunteered to keep his grandchildren overnight so his daughter and her husband, Aaron, could go out to dinner for their anniversary. He joined Finn on the couch, smiling when his sleepy grandson crawled over and curled up next to him. He lightly tapped on Finn's hand as Riley had asked him to do whenever Finn started sucking his thumb.

Clearly that was Riley's technique because the second he

touched Finn's hand, the young boy pulled his thumb out without comment or thought. The action brought to mind an old Irish folktale and it occurred to Pat, he'd never told his grandson the tale.

"Did I ever tell you the story of Finn MacCool?" Patrick asked.

Finn lifted his head. The boy loved a good story. "He has my name?"

"He does, indeed," Patrick said. "And he was known as the greatest man in all of Ireland."

"Why?"

"Oh, well, that's a fine story. It has to do with a salmon and thumb sucking."

Finn crinkled his nose. "I don't like salmon. Mommy makes me eat it because it's good for me."

Patrick chuckled. "It *is* good for you." Finn would exist solely on tater tots and chicken nuggets if he had his way. "And maybe you'll change your mind when you realize that, in this story, the salmon—who was still alive and swimming around—had all the knowledge in the world."

Finn was obviously unimpressed, and Patrick realized he was focusing on the wrong things. "Let me start over," he said, beginning again. "Once upon a time, there was a brave warrior named Finn MacCool. It is said he was the best man that ever walked on the green grass of Ireland."

"He was a warrior?" That had gotten Finn's attention.

Patrick nodded. "One of the most courageous warriors ever. As the story goes, when Finn was just a young boy, he was hidden away from his family to protect him from them and sent to live with druids."

"His family wanted to hurt him?"

"I'm sad to say they did. His grandfather didn't approve of his daughter marrying Finn's father."

"So he had a mean Pop Pop who made him eat his green beans and let his sister watch that stupid princess movie instead of playing video games?" From the mischievous grin on his grandson's face, it was apparent Finn was getting a kick out of teasing Patrick for all the things he'd done today.

Patrick chuckled, tickling Finn. "He did, ye wee rascal, so you best take care, lest we send you off to live with the druids as well."

"What's a droo—drood?"

"Religious leaders."

Finn crinkled his nose again. "The Finn in this story had to sit through church every day? Not just on Sunday?"

Finn was not a fan of sitting still...in any environment. Though the preacher's sermon each week appeared to be the most taxing on the lad.

"I suppose he did."

"Poor Finn MacCool." Finn rested his head on Patrick's shoulder again. He was such an affectionate, clever young boy, always laughing, always happy. Patrick wrapped his arm around Finn's shoulders.

"One day, he was fishing with one of the druids, when the older man caught the Salmon of Knowledge."

"Did he make Finn eat it?"

Patrick ruffled the little boy's hair. "Actually," he started, "he told him *not* to eat the fish."

Finn lifted a victorious fist in the air, the way he'd obviously seen the grown men in the family do whenever the Ravens scored a touchdown. "Yes! I like this droo...drood."

"Don't get too excited yet," Patrick warned. "The druid told Finn not to eat the salmon because *he* wanted it, wanted the knowledge that he'd receive."

"What's knowledge?" Finn asked.

Patrick had wondered if his young grandson understood that part. "That's the magic part of this tale. This salmon knew everything."

"Everything? Like in the whole world?"

Patrick nodded.

"Did the salmon know how to play Super Mario? Could he beat all the levels?"

Patrick worked hard to keep a straight face as he said, "Absolutely."

"Wow. Can salmon help me do that?"

Patrick was sorely tempted to tell the little white lie, simply to encourage his grandson to try healthier foods. Then he heard his beloved Sunday's voice in his head, saying what she always used to say when their young ones wouldn't eat their vegetables. "They'll discover what they like and dislike in life on their own. Forcing them won't change that."

Still, he fudged a little. "I'm not sure it will help you beat *all* the levels, but...it might help. It is a brain food."

Finn considered that. And immediately dismissed it. "I still don't like salmon."

Patrick chuckled. Score one for Sunday. Then he continued his story. "Regardless, you can see why the druid wanted to keep the salmon to himself. Beating all the Mario levels is a very important skill. So he charged Finn with cooking the fish, warning him not to eat it. Finn did as he was told because he was a good, honest, kind boy—"

"And because salmon is yucky."

Patrick grinned at the interruption. "However, as he was getting ready to serve the fish to the old man, some grease got on him and burned Finn's thumb. Because it hurt, he put his thumb in his mouth and sucked it. And what do you think happened then?"

"His mommy told him to stop?"

Patrick shook his head, fighting hard not to laugh. Finn was a rascal. "No. All that knowledge that the salmon had flew right into Finn's head—and suddenly he knew *everything*."

"Hooray for Finn! He got smart *and* he didn't have to eat the fish. I like that story."

Patrick ruffled his grandson's hair playfully. "You wee scamp. You know, you aren't that much different from that Finn who lived all those hundreds of years ago. You're brave and smart and a good boy."

Finn curled up on Patrick's lap, resting his head on his chest sleepily. "You tell good stories."

Patrick placed a soft kiss to the top of the boy's head. "Thank you."

"I'm going to be a great man too."

Patrick smiled. "I'm certain you will be. The greatest man in all of Baltimore."

Finn lifted his head, shaking it. "I can't be that, Pop Pop."

"Why not?"

"Because you are."

Patrick's heart swelled with love as he wrapped his arms around the young boy until he fell asleep.

He remained on the couch for a good hour afterwards, just holding Finn.

And smiling.

1

Finn balled up a piece of paper and lobbed it across the room, raising his hands and proclaiming, "Two points!" as he hit the trash can.

Fergus looked up from his computer and rolled his eyes. "Thought you were going to work on payroll today."

Finn glanced outside the window and sighed. The sun was shining, but not hotly, as the humidity of summer had finally burned off. The sky was so bright and blue and cloudless, it made it impossible for him to sit inside. September had arrived and brought cooler weather that had him longing for nights by a fire pit, candy corn mixed with peanuts, and hot apple cider with caramel vodka. Fall was his favorite season.

"It's too nice a day to be trapped inside."

"You're hardly tied to the chair, Finn. You can go outside whenever you want."

"The problem with that is, you're going to expect me to come back inside eventually."

Fergus chuckled and started typing on his laptop again. Business at Collins Security had picked up in the past couple of months, thanks to Fergus. He'd served as Aubrey Summers's bodyguard on her last tour, saving her life from a dangerous stalker. His cousin had impressed the powers-that-be at a large local concert venue, and they'd just landed a huge contract that placed Collins Security in charge of all their event security. As such, they'd been busting their asses the past few weeks, hiring and training staff, doing detailed analysis of the layout of the concert hall, searching for weaknesses in security.

Finn was thrilled that their business venture was turning out to be so successful. Before Fergus had returned from two stints in the Army, Finn had been wandering around somewhat aimlessly, clueless. He'd been pursuing a business degree, but he'd had no idea what he wanted to do with it. When Fergus suggested they go into business together, it had seemed like the answer to a prayer, and he loved basically being his own boss.

What he didn't like was pulling six twelve-hour days a week. Or working inside on a beautiful fall day.

He looked outside once more and sighed.

Fergus didn't glance up, though he clearly heard him. "Go across the street and get a cup of coffee. Take a break for a little while."

Finn stood up and stretched. It was a good suggestion. Maybe he'd even take a stroll around the block a couple of times to soak up some vitamin D. "You want anything?"

Fergus shook his head and lifted his water bottle. "I'm good."

Finn walked down the two flights of stairs, stopping briefly to say hello to a couple of women who worked in the real estate office on the floor beneath them, before stepping out onto the sidewalk.

They'd set up shop on the third floor of a business office near the waterfront. Fergus had liked the location, given its close proximity to downtown. Finn had liked that they were walking distance from his apartment above Pat's Pub and the fact his favorite coffee shop was right across the street.

The bell above the door tinkled when Finn walked in, sucking in a long, deep breath of fresh-brewed coffee and pastries. Daily Grind had the best coffee in the city, and they made the most delicious scones he'd ever eaten, though he'd never tell his mother that.

Mom, along with his cousin Yvonne, was the chef at Pat's Pub, the restaurant/bar his family had owned and operated for decades. Riley insisted that her scones were the best in the city, and Finn had enough sense not to contradict her.

Even though she was wrong.

He glanced at the handwritten specials to see what today's featured coffee blend was. It was mid-morning and he was the only one in the place. The rush was over as everyone had already grabbed their early-morning jolt and headed on to work. The place would crowd up again at lunchtime because the coffee shop also sold wonderful sandwiches and wraps.

A woman walked out from the back, wiping her hands with a towel and smiling. "I'm sorry to keep you wait—Finn Young?"

Finn looked at the woman, his eyes widening when recognition dawned. "LJ?"

Layla Jean Moretti stepped around the counter as he lifted his arms, the two of them hugging. "Oh my God. No one has called me LJ since elementary school. I'm just Layla now. I haven't seen you since…"

"Since we were eleven," he finished for her. Layla had grown up since then—and he was blown away by how beautiful she was. Tall and lithe, with porcelain skin and chocolate-brown eyes, she took his breath away.

She'd always been the prettiest girl in their class, with her long, wavy brown hair and dark eyes, but that hadn't really sparked his eleven-year-old boy interest. In elementary school, the only way Layla would have garnered his attention was if she'd been able to transform into a Pokémon.

"God, it's great to see you."

"How's your dad? Your brothers?" he asked. He and Layla had been classmates right up until the summer after sixth grade, when her mother died of cancer and her dad packed up Layla and her siblings and moved them to Philadelphia, where he had family who could help him raise his five kids.

"They're great. I mean, my brothers are still annoying-as-hell, overprotective bastards, but it's not like that's ever going to change."

Finn laughed. Layla, like him, came from a very large, loud, boisterous family. She was the youngest and only daughter, which meant she had four big brothers who had doted on her, while she'd given them a run for their money. "So what you're saying is, you're still spoiled rotten."

"Absolutely. As I should be."

"What are you doing here?" Finn asked.

"I moved back and bought myself a coffee shop."

"You bought this shop?"

She nodded. "Yep. The previous owner retired."

"I had no idea Mr. Shepley was selling the business."

"It wasn't really advertised. He and my papa remained really good friends even after we moved. He visited us in Philly a few months ago and mentioned that he was thinking about selling the store and retiring to Florida. How cliché is that?" she joked. "Anyway, he and I struck up a conversation and made a deal. He never even put it on the market. Mama had set up a trust fund for me and my brothers before she passed, and I decided to take the money and escape Philly and the boys."

Finn grinned. "Your brothers are great guys, LJ."

"Of course they are, when you deal with them singly. But when all four of them get together, it's hard work. I decided I needed a fresh start in a city where there weren't four Moretti brothers breathing down my neck."

"How long have you been back in Baltimore?"

"Four weeks. Spent the first two weeks finding and setting up my apartment, and the last two learning the ropes of the coffee business from Mr. Shepley."

Finn had been in the shop only twice in the past couple of weeks as he and Fergus had been working across town at the event venue, doing security checks. He hadn't seen her or Mr. Shepley on those visits.

"How many times have your brothers visited since you moved?" he asked.

Layla laughed. "Three times. They're insane. But I put the kibosh on their constant trips down here during the last visit. Told them the next time I was willing to see them was at Thanksgiving. Not that I expect that to stick." She walked back around the counter. "What are you doing right now? Working? Have time to catch up over a cup of coffee?"

Finn nodded, and then pointed across the street to his office building. "I've got some time. I work right over there. Third floor. Started a security firm with my cousin, Fergus."

"No way. That's so awesome. So what's your poison?" she asked, pointing to the menu.

"Coffee the way God intended. Black and strong with none of that fancy shit in it."

Layla clutched her chest. "A man after my own heart." She poured them both a cup of coffee. She added milk to hers, and then the two of them sat down at one of the tables.

"How's *your* family?" she asked.

"Same as yours. Still crazy."

"And your Pop Pop?"

"Still holding court at the pub, even though he's retired. My uncle Tris and cousin Padraig run the bar now, and my mom is cooking up a storm on Sunday's Side."

Layla blew the steam off her coffee. "I love hearing that your Pop Pop is still doing well. Your family was the best. I'm going to have to swing by the pub to see everyone. Landon still around?"

Layla had been a bit of a tomboy when they were growing up. How could she not be with so many brothers? So she'd raced around the playground with him and his best friend, Landon, at recess rather than hanging with the girls by the swing set talking about...whatever ten-year-old girls talked about.

"Oh my God, are you ready for this? Landon is marrying Sunnie."

"Your *sister*?" Layla grinned.

Finn shrugged. "They went viral a year ago."

"Viral?"

"Ever seen the video, 'Hot Cop Saves Sexy Nurse'?"

"Shut. Up." Layla shoved Finn's shoulder playfully. "That was them? I had no idea." She glanced around. "I'm going to have to look that up on YouTube as soon as I remember where I put my phone."

"I'm back from break," a male voice called from the back room.

Layla turned around and waved as one of her employees took his station behind the counter. "Great. Do you mind making another pot of decaf, Seth? I didn't have time."

"No problem." Seth started working as she turned back to him.

"It really is great to see you, Finn."

"Same." Finn glanced outside, reluctant to cut their reunion short. "What are you doing tonight?" he asked.

Layla shrugged. "Not much. Usually I just work here until close, then head home for a late dinner."

"Wanna go out with me? We can catch up over a late dinner or drinks at the pub."

"Okay," she said. "That would be fun. What time?"

"What time do you close?" he asked.

"Eight."

"Perfect. Want me to pick you up here or at your place?"

"How about my place at eight thirty? I'd love to change clothes first. Otherwise, I'll smell like coffee all night."

Finn grinned. "You say that like it's a bad thing. Here," he handed his phone over, "put your number in my contacts. I'll text you and you can send me your address."

Layla took his phone and added her number. He grinned when she listed her name as LJ. He was never going to get the hang of calling her Layla and it didn't look like she cared if he didn't.

The bell rang as a couple who looked like tourists walked in. Layla handed him his phone as she stood. "Guess I should get back to work."

"Me too. I'm sort of surprised Fergus hasn't already texted me to ask where the hell I am." As if he'd summoned the text, Finn's phone pinged. Glancing at the screen, he laughed, then turned the display to show her Fergus's text that simply said, "Coming back?"

She giggled, and then gave him another hug. Finn wrapped his arms around her and tried to ignore the way his body warmed as her breasts pressed against his chest, her soft hair tickled his cheek. Suddenly the smell of coffee was a pretty potent aphrodisiac.

Layla stepped away...and it occurred to him she'd felt something as well when he saw her blush, smiling at him shyly.

He let his hands fall away.

"See you later."

He nodded. "Later, LJ."

Damn. So much for taking a walk so he could refocus himself.

Now he was more distracted than ever.

FOUR HOURS LATER, FINN WAS STARING UNSEEINGLY AT THE computer screen. He'd gotten fuck-all done as he played over his conversation with Layla, recalling how her whole face lit up when she laughed. The attraction he'd felt toward her was instant and powerful.

Ever since opening the business with Fergus, they'd been pulling long hours. Finn hadn't gone out on more than a handful of dates, always too tired at the end of the day. That wasn't going to be true tonight. With each passing hour, he felt more energized, excited.

He knew this technically wasn't a date, just two old friends going out to reminisce, reconnect.

So it was the height of foolishness for him to wonder what it would feel like to wrap those long strands of soft hair around his fingers, tugging it until her face lifted so he could lower his lips to hers and—

"Jesus Christ, man. Go home already," Fergus interrupted just before he got to the good part.

"Sorry."

"I thought the coffee would wake you up, but it looks like it did the opposite."

Finn told Fergus he'd run into an old friend from elementary school at the coffee shop, but Fergus had gotten a call before he could say who, so Finn had gone back to his desk and continued to fail at work.

"I think I'm going to call today a wash."

Fergus leaned back in his desk chair, and Finn noticed his cousin looked wiped out. "It's okay. We've been pulling some long hours. I think I'm going to knock off early too. Aubrey's coming home tonight, and I want to clean up the apartment."

Fergus had fallen head over heels in love with pop star Aubrey Summers when he was serving as her bodyguard. After saving her from a stalker, the two of them had found an apartment together nearby, which meant Fergus had moved out of the Collins Dorm—the name his mother had given the apartment he currently shared with his cousin, Colm and his sister, Darcy.

When Aubrey's concert tour ended on the Fourth of July, she'd remained in Baltimore with Fergus, writing songs for her next album. She'd left late last week to do a few shows on the West Coast, and while she'd only been gone five days, Fergus acted as if they'd been apart for years.

"She's not going to give a shit if the apartment is clean as long as there are sheets on the bed," Finn joked.

"There's a good chance we won't make it to the bedroom."

Finn held up his hand to cut off the conversation. "Spare me the details of your well-laid life. It's been just me and my hand for too fucking long, dude."

Fergus laughed. "You need to find yourself a girl and succumb to the Collins curse."

"The curse has nothing to do with it. I just want sex."

Which was a lie. For a long time, that *was* what Finn wanted, to live footloose and fancy-free, to hang on to his single status for as long as he could before settling down and committing himself to one woman for the rest of his life.

But not anymore.

Their cousin Colm, the eternal bachelor in the Collins family, swore there was a curse hanging over all their heads that meant when they least expected or wanted it, love swept in, taking them all down hard and fast. Finn used to laugh at the concept, but as more and more of his family members went down—finding their true loves and moving out of the apartment—he was starting to believe there was some truth to what Colm considered dire warnings.

Yvonne had been the latest casualty. His cousin had recently fallen for Leo, a single dad, and she'd been spending every night at his place for weeks. He figured it was just a matter of time before she managed to move all her stuff over to Leo's. Finn didn't like to think about how quiet the apartment would be then.

Truthfully, lately Finn found himself wishing the curse would come for him. He was surrounded by couples in love, and damn if they didn't make it look pretty freaking awesome.

Unfortunately, with the business taking off, he barely had enough time to scratch his ass these days, thanks to the increased workload. So it wasn't like dating was on the table at the moment. Or, at least, that was what he told himself every night when he climbed into his empty bed, trying not to think about how lonely he was.

"Good luck with finding a hookup then. Though I have to tell you, you're missing out on something pretty awesome,"

Fergus said, shutting down his computer and stretching as he stood.

"Says the guy sleeping with Aubrey Summers, my teenage crush. I figure she was responsible for eighty percent of my wet dre—"

"Gonna stop you there," Fergus cut in. "After all, you're talking about my future wife."

"I knew her first," Finn grumbled.

Fergus laughed. "Being a member of her fan club in seventh grade doesn't count."

Finn grinned and turned off his computer, slipping his cell phone into his back pocket. The other benefit to this job was, on days when they didn't have meetings, he and Fergus adopted a casual dress code, which meant he wasn't forced to give up his blue jeans in favor of a suit and tie every day.

He and Fergus locked up the office and walked downstairs together. At the sidewalk, they went in opposite directions.

"Say hey to Miguel for me," Fergus said, by way of a goodbye. "I'll hop back in with you guys next week."

Finn waved, realizing his cousin would think he was going to see Miguel tonight. After all, the three of them had a standing Wednesday night meeting at the Collins Dorm. Miguel Garcia, a Baltimore cop and his best friend, and Fergus came to the dorm every Wednesday to teach Finn defensive tactics, as he hoped to start spending more time out in the field and less behind a desk at Collins Security. So far, he was pretty solidly terrible at everything they'd taught him, something that amused Fergus and Miguel way too much.

Fergus had canceled tonight to be with Aubrey, and now he was going to have to do the same.

He pulled out his cell and hit Miguel's number.

"What's up, bro?" Miguel said as he answered.

"Hey, listen, I'm going to have to bail on tonight."

"Oh yeah? Get a better offer?" Miguel asked.

Finn laughed. "Hell yeah. Ran into an old friend from

elementary school, LJ. We're going out tonight to catch up over drinks. Figure that beats sweating my ass off as you beat the shit out of me."

Miguel chuckled. "Dude. We've been at it for months. You should be kicking *my* ass by now."

Finn grimaced. He was no slouch in the muscles department and he was a pretty big guy, just like his dad and uncles. None of that was worth a damn compared to Miguel, who was built like a brick shit house. There wasn't an ounce of fat anywhere on the man. Probably because when he wasn't chasing down bad guys on the job, he was lifting weights at the gym or going on ten-mile runs just for the fun of it. Who the fuck did that?

"One of these days, I'm going to take you down," Finn declared. "So rain check on tonight?"

"Yeah. No problem. I might put in a few extra hours at the precinct. Been a couple of robberies downtown, local businesses hit. We can't catch the guy. Your dad put me in charge of the case today."

Miguel worked under Finn's dad, Aaron, on the police force. He knew Miguel was hoping to make sergeant when the next round of promotions came out, something Dad also knew. Clearly he was hoping to give Miguel a chance to prove himself and earn some brownie points.

"Nice," Finn said. "Closing a case like that would look good."

"I know. Have a good time with your old friend tonight. You guys drink one for me, okay?"

"You got it."

Finn hung up and continued walking to the pub, glancing out over the water, considering his conversation with Miguel. It was obvious his best friend thought LJ was a male. And he hadn't corrected the assumption.

Why hadn't he?

Finn pulled up short and walked over to the railing, staring off across the harbor. Well...he knew why, but it wasn't something he'd been able to successfully wrap his head around in any clear fashion.

Miguel was bisexual. Finn had known that since the first time they'd met, and truthfully, he didn't give two shits who Miguel slept with. That was his friend's business. His parents and godmother, Bubbles, had raised him with one simple motto: Live and let live.

Miguel was a great guy and one of the best friends Finn had ever had. They'd met when Miguel was partnered up with Landon on the police force two years earlier, and the two of them had really clicked. They had the same off-color sense of humor and irreverence for anything serious. They rooted for the same sports teams, listened to the same music, and were attracted to the same type of females. They connected on everything right down the line, and while Finn had lots of friends and close cousins, there was something that set Miguel apart from the others, that drew Finn in just a little bit closer.

He hadn't realized what it was until a few months ago. And when he did?

Fuck.

Finn had been struggling ever since.

He and Miguel had gone with a bunch of guys to Houston for Landon's bachelor party. In true stag night fashion, they'd all gotten a little—okay, a lot—shit-faced. Miguel had started flirting with Finn, which wasn't unusual. He was used to Miguel making jokes about his tight ass or Justin Timberlake hairstyle, and he'd always figured it was his best friend's way of trying to get a rise out of him. Just another way to tease him.

But that night, Miguel had let his guard down...and for just a moment, the flirting felt serious. Real.

There'd been a glancing touch, a look that revealed way too much.

Finn had panicked and played it off like he always did, pretending to think it was all a big joke, and Miguel had rebounded quickly, putting them back on the path of "just buds."

But Finn hadn't been able to forget that look, that touch.

Or the way they had made him feel.

"I'm straight," he mumbled, feeling like a jackass for talking to himself. He liked women. He *really* liked women. He always had. He'd never once glanced at a guy and felt an attraction. Never. Not once.

Until July.

Now, he wasn't sure *what* he felt.

He loved Miguel like a brother, so was that messing with his head? Was that making him think he was feeling an attraction when it was really just affection?

He pushed away from the railing and started for his apartment, doing the same thing he'd done for two months. He shoved away his confusion over Miguel and turned his thoughts to something simpler.

LJ. Layla.

He grinned as he thought about seeing her again, ignoring the tiny voice in the back of his head that said he should have told Miguel his old friend was a woman.

2

Layla laughed so hard she snorted as she and Finn reminisced about elementary school. They'd gone out to dinner six times over the past couple of weeks. Finding him again had been the answer to a prayer, as he'd reintroduced her to the city, pointing out all the things that had changed as well as the things that were the same.

They'd eaten at his family's pub a couple of times, and she'd been welcomed into their fold like some prodigal daughter. She had been thrilled to reconnect with Landon and Sunnie and Darcy, as well as hang out with Finn's other cousins, some she'd known well, some she'd never met.

One night, Finn's Pop Pop had joined them for dinner, asking about her family. She had remembered Mr. Collins quite fondly from when she was a kid. He had come to her house a couple of times before her mama died, and then quite a few times after the funeral, helping Layla's papa cope with the loss. Mr. Collins, like Papa, had lost his wife to cancer when his children were young. He'd helped Papa through the weeks following Mama's death.

Even now, Papa, good Italian Catholic that he was, was ready to put Mr. Collins's name in for sainthood.

"All I'm saying is, I taught you a valuable lesson that day," Layla joked. "Always protect the crown jewels."

Finn shook his head, his grin wide. He had a gorgeous smile. God, he had a gorgeous everything. She'd never thought herself a fan of beards, but there was no denying Finn looked hot as hell with his. It made him look rugged, lumberjack sexy.

"I'm lucky there's anything left to protect. Seriously, LJ. You emasculated me with that damn kickball."

She shrugged unapologetically. "I've always been too competitive for my own good."

"A Moretti trait, for sure," he said, agreeing.

"Absolutely. The Morettis are feisty, fierce, competitive, passionate. And we totally own it. I'm sure your family has similar traits that run through the whole lot of you."

"Hmmm," Finn mused. "Now that you mention it…I guess if I had to describe us, I'd say the Collinses are laid-back, crazy, fun partiers who don't take life too seriously. Oh, and we're a bunch of hopeless romantics."

"Romantics, huh? Present company included?" she asked.

Finn shook his head. "No. I'd say I should be excluded."

Layla didn't believe that. "Excluded from the romantic part or the hopeless part, because I'm going to have to disagree on that last one."

He grinned. "Smart-ass. But yeah. Both. My cousin Colm is determined to escape the curse that's befallen most of the other Collinses. Padraig, Fergus, Lochlan, hell, even Landon—the honorary Collins—have fallen fast and hard. You should see those guys. Head over ass in love with their women, the whole lot of them. Except…"

A shadow fell over his face for a moment.

"Except?"

"Well, Padraig's wife, Mia, passed away a couple of years ago. Not that he stopped loving her. Truth is, he's still struggling to get over her death."

Padraig was one of the cousins Layla hadn't known because

he'd been older than her and Finn, several grades ahead of them in school. She'd met him at the pub earlier in the week and really liked him. Hell, she liked all of Finn's family. He hadn't been wrong when he'd called them easygoing and fun. "Oh no. I'm sorry. She must have been terribly young."

Finn nodded. "Brain tumor."

Layla reached out, resting her hand on top of Finn's. "I'm so sorry to hear that."

"Mia was amazing. I really liked her, and I know it's been tough on Padraig. He hasn't dated anyone since she died, and part of me is worried he'll never be able to move on, never find anyone else."

Layla gave him a smile. "And you say you're not romantic."

Finn chuckled, even as he rolled his eyes. "Fine. I'll prove it to you. I've never had a serious girlfriend. My dating history is filled with casual hookups, one-night stands, and the occasional month-long lust affair."

Layla sighed. "Sounds like bliss."

Finn barked out a loud laugh. "Seriously?"

"Hell yeah. At least, you've had some adventure, some passion, some variety. Meanwhile, I've spent the last five years in a too-serious relationship with the guy I lost my virginity to."

Finn frowned. "I didn't realize you had a—"

She recognized his confusion and hastened to add, "We broke up a few months ago."

"Is that what prompted the move back to Baltimore?"

She nodded. "That was a big part of it. My brothers loved Marco, and they were convinced the two of us were going to get married and give them lots of nieces and nephews."

"What went wrong?"

Layla lifted one shoulder. "My brothers loved him more than I did. Don't get me wrong. Marco is a great guy. Nice, reliable, handsome, and I did love him." She paused and corrected herself. "I *do* love him. As a friend. I just wasn't *in* love with him.

Our relationship had become really boring, extremely predictable.

"A few months ago, we went out to dinner together at one of our favorite restaurants. Right before dessert, Marco pulled out an engagement ring and proposed. There were flowers on the table, candlelight, soft music playing. Super romantic, right?"

Finn nodded. "Textbook, I'd say."

"Exactly. It was like he'd Googled 'romantic proposals' and checked all the boxes because the true nature of our relationship was more like comfortable friends rather than passionate lovers. I swear I looked at that ring for what felt like forever, letting our future together play out in my mind. I tried to imagine our honeymoon, and all I could see us doing was flying to some tropical paradise where we'd sip fruity drinks and then fall into bed before ten...no sex, no dancing, no swinging from the chandeliers."

Finn chuckled. "I could see you swinging from light fixtures."

"I rejected the proposal. And you want to know the crazy part?"

"Sure."

"I think Marco was relieved. I'm pretty sure he'd only proposed because that felt like the next logical step. Five years is a long time, and like I said, we weren't bad together. We just weren't madly in love."

"How did your brothers take it?"

She rolled her eyes. "Like they take everything, the hot-blooded Italians. They flipped out, tried to convince me I'd made a mistake. Started listing all of Marco's fine attributes."

"What are they?" Finn asked.

"The typical things that big brothers like in potential husbands for their sister. He had a good job, was reliable, respectful. Rooted for the right sports teams, didn't drink too much and he'd never stray. Plus, Marco was perfectly happy in Philadelphia, which is where my brothers plan to live out the rest of their lives. Marco always said he was born there and he'd die there, and while Philly is fine, I wasn't as keen to live three minutes away from twenty-seven family members for the rest of my life."

Finn took a sip of his beer and lifted one shoulder. "You know, your brothers' list doesn't sound that bad."

"Marco roots for the Eagles."

"The man is a monster. You made a lucky break."

Layla grinned briefly, but just thinking of Marco fired up the same frustration she'd felt since moving to Baltimore. She leaned back in her chair and sighed. "It's just…I can't help but think I've missed out on a lot of hot, meaningless sex. I got out from under my brothers' thumbs after high school only to revoke that freedom by settling down with," she sighed, "Marco. I feel like there's this whole slutty side of me that's been overlooked while I've been going through the motions with Marco."

"Oooookay," Finn drawled. "Slutty, huh? Is that seriously what you want?"

"For right now? Yes. Absolutely. I want exactly what you described. Casual, no-strings. I've been reading a lot of dirty books and watching a shit ton of porn. I have a million kinky things I want to try."

"Trying to decide if that's TMI or not enough information. Because when you say kinky—"

She held up her hand to cut him off. "This is a family restaurant."

Finn laughed, then shook his head. "You know, LJ, there's a lot to be said for solid, comfortable relationships. I mean, the hookups are fun for about five minutes, but then—"

Layla feigned a horrified face at his time limit, which prompted a laugh and a quick backtrack. "Well, two, three hours, at least. Twelve hours, if we're talking about me, but I know I'm not most men."

She giggled. "But then?"

"But then, at the end of the night, I'm back home, alone in my bed."

"So correct me if I'm wrong, Mr. Hopeless Romantic, but it sounds like you want a relationship, want to succumb to the curse."

Finn fell silent, and she could see she'd hit the nail on the head.

"Yeah. I do." He paused, then nodded. "I want what Fergus has. A girlfriend, someone to come home to every night, someone to split pizzas and fight over the remote with."

"I had all that. And believe me, I feel lucky to have gotten out." She picked up a breadstick, toying with it rather than eating. His confession confirmed what she'd known after just a few minutes of conversation with Finn that first day in the coffee shop. He was a good guy. A nice guy. And she was thrilled they'd been able to pick up their friendship where they'd left off all those years ago in middle school.

But it also depressed her. Because she'd come to Baltimore with solid goals, and ever since running into Finn at the coffee shop, she had started playing out not just-friends' fantasies with him in her head.

Now, she panicked a little, thinking maybe he'd considered all these nights with her dates, when she'd been careful to keep them in the friends' zone, not wanting to blur the lines.

He took a sip of his beer. "This sounds like one of those 'grass is always greener on the other side' debates."

"So you want a girlfriend. There's nothing wrong with that," she said. "I think you should go for it. Not to inflate your already too-large ego, but I'm sure there are a million girls in Baltimore who'd love to date you."

The heated look he gave her said she was right to start this conversation. Especially when he said, "Maybe, maybe not. Right now, work is kicking my ass, so dating doesn't really seem like an option."

She shook her head. "That's a poor excuse, and I don't believe it. I mean, you've managed to find time to go out with me half a dozen nights in the last couple weeks."

"True."

Layla sipped her wine, trying to figure out a way to let Finn down easy...if his thoughts about dating had turned to her. She couldn't be what he wanted. Not right now anyway. And not for a long time. She'd vowed to give herself one unentangled year. "Maybe we can help each other. I can be your wingman, help you meet women with more than sex on their minds."

Finn stroked his beard, considering her offer. "That's a nice offer, but I don't know how I feel about helping you hook up with strangers. Especially now that I know you've got kinky, slutty plans for them. I mean, I like to think of myself as a pretty generous, selfless guy, but I'm not *that* selfless."

Layla laughed. "I think we've just determined that you and I can't happen. You want more than I'm ready to give. I moved here to explore my wild side. No more boyfriends for me. Just casual, set-the-sheets-on-fire sex with no day-after phone calls."

"Yeah? You know what? Fuck it. I've changed my mind on wanting a relationship. They're totally overrated."

She cast her eyes upward and grinned. "I'm sure they aren't... with the right person."

"Your wild side, huh?" Finn clearly liked the sound of that, but before they could discuss it further, the waiter showed up with their food. They'd hit a new Italian place she'd been wanting to try.

They started eating and the conversation returned to more reminiscing, as they talked about fellow classmates they'd run into over the years.

After they paid the bill, they walked to the parking lot together. Layla tried to resist the pull to kiss Finn. She'd been gone long enough that she didn't really have a lot of friends in Baltimore, and while she'd been busy this first month and a half, setting up her apartment and working at the store, she had experienced more than her fair share of loneliness.

Not that that was surprising, really. In Philadelphia, she'd lived at home with her papa, her brothers constantly in and out of the house. Her aunt and uncle and their huge brood lived right next door, and they were always over. And if she wasn't at home, she was at Marco's apartment with him. So it was a rarity for Layla to ever be alone.

In Baltimore, except for when she was at the coffee shop or with Finn or when her brothers visited, she'd been completely on her own, which she was surprised to discover she didn't like as much as she'd thought she might. She was a social person, and she genuinely liked people. Eating, watching TV, and going to the grocery store alone kinda sucked, but she figured that was something she just needed to get used to.

One year. No entanglements. That vow had become her mantra.

"Wanna come over to watch the football game with us on Sunday?" Finn asked.

She nodded. "Yeah. I'd love to."

His invitation solidified the fact that she'd be pretty freaking stupid to come on to Finn. He and his family were the perfect Baltimore friends for her. Actually, they were currently her *only* Baltimore friends.

They were fun and active and always inviting her to do cool stuff. She and Sunnie had made plans to go to lunch one day next week, and there was talk of a Halloween party and other annual traditions they all seemed more than happy to include her in. Throwing all that away for a hookup would be a huge mistake. Especially since a hookup was all it could be.

They got into Finn's car, and he cranked up the radio, the two of them singing along to the nineties station, Layla amused by how many of the words Finn knew.

When they pulled up in front of her apartment, she was surprised when he parked the car. "You don't have to get out. I'm perfectly capable of walking myself up to the third floor."

Finn turned the car off, then shifted in his seat to face her. "Let's talk about that wild side thing again."

"Finn," she laughed. "You and I are in different places in our lives at the moment."

"I'm *very* good at casual sex."

Layla's previous resolve wavered. Her sex life with Marco had been...missionary. At the beginning, they'd had a lot of sex and she'd enjoyed it, vanilla as it was. But then, her sleepovers at his place turned into just that. Nine times out of ten, they'd just sleep together in the same bed, sex the exception rather than the rule. And even then, the sex had gotten as predictable and boring as the relationship.

Finn looked like the kind of guy who knew his way around the bedroom and she was super attracted to him. But there was something in his eyes, something in the way he looked at her, that told her he hadn't really accepted what she'd said about not wanting a relationship.

"I'm sure you are. With strangers. We're friends, Finn. What happens after the sex? We just go back to being friends?"

"Sure."

"Are *you* sure?" she stressed.

"LJ. I'm not sure what you're getting at."

"What if another guy asks me out and I accept? You'd be alright with me dating other guys? Sleeping with other guys? Because that's what I want to do."

Finn didn't reply, but she thought perhaps her words were beginning to sink in. Then he gave her a wicked grin. "I'm pretty sure you wouldn't want to sleep with anyone after me. I'd ruin you for all other men."

She laughed as she threw her head back and rolled her eyes. "Oh my God. Well, that solves that problem. I simply can't risk it, Finn. I have a lot of wild oats to sow, and I can't take the chance that you'll ruin my good time."

"I love hanging out with you, LJ. These past couple weeks have been a lot of fun. And I get what you're saying. I really do." He grinned, but there was a part of her that didn't think he looked particularly happy.

"So...we're just going to stay friends."

"Sure. Friends."

Layla noticed his easy smile had faded and she hated it. "So, we're cool?" she asked, feeling the need for reassurance.

He nodded. "We're cool."

Layla leaned toward him, giving him a hug. Part of her was tempted to turn her head and add a kiss to the embrace, despite what she'd just said. Because she'd had some rather lustful fantasies of him lately. Her current favorite was the two of them re-envisioning childhood games they used to play. Playing doctor and cops and robbers with a kinky twist.

She pushed herself away and hoped Finn couldn't see the blush she felt heating her cheeks. "Call me tomorrow?"

He winked. "Absolutely, friend."

They said goodbye and Layla climbed the stairs to her apartment. But later, in bed, she closed her eyes and gave in to the fantasies, imagining Finn tying her to the bed, using her vibrator on her, teasing her, keeping her right on the edge of an orgasm for hours, before allowing her to come.

As she drifted off to sleep, she couldn't help but suspect Finn might be right. He *was* starting to ruin her for other men.

And he hadn't touched her anywhere but in her fantasies.

❧　3　❧

A few days later, Finn sat at the bar at Pat's Pub alone, wondering what to do about Layla and her wild side. He hadn't seen her since the night she'd expressed her desire to explore her wild side. One of her employees had quit, and she'd had to pick up the extra shifts while trying to hire and train someone new.

If he'd been working at the office, he would have stopped by the shop to see her, but he and Fergus had been onsite, tightening down security for a local concert his cousin-in-law Hunter Maxwell was doing over the weekend.

"Hello, my lad."

Finn grinned as Pop Pop claimed the stool next to him. "I didn't know you were here," he said.

Pop Pop nodded when Padraig walked over with a frosty mug and pointed to the Guinness tap. "That would be wonderful, Paddy," he said, before turning back to Finn. "I was having dinner on Sunday's Side with Caitlyn and Lucas. Tonight's special was Riley's shepherd's pie. You know that's my favorite." Pop Pop patted his stomach. "Though perhaps I shouldn't indulge in it as often as I do."

His grandfather was in good shape for his age. Actually, Finn thought it looked like he'd lost a bit of weight in the past year or so, not that he'd ever mention that to Pop Pop, or anyone else for that matter. Pop Pop was over ninety, and Finn preferred to think of his beloved grandfather as immortal.

"You're the best-looking guy in here," Finn said, glancing over to the end of the bar where Emmy, a romance writer, had set up camp the past month or two to write her latest book. "Isn't that right, Emmy?"

She glanced up and grinned. "Not even a contest, Mr. Collins. You are a serious heartthrob."

Pop Pop was clearly pleased by the compliment. "Emmy, dear. I've told you countless times to call me Pat. And I'm not sure how you can write those stories of yours while listening to everything everyone around you is saying."

Emmy laughed and winked. "What can I say? Eavesdropping is my one true talent."

Padraig set the Guinness in front of Pop Pop, joining the conversation. "Eavesdropping? Not writing?"

"I have to work at the writing," Emmy said. "The eavesdropping comes naturally."

"Woman after my own heart," Pop Pop, the nosiest man alive, joked.

Padraig laughed, then went to take the orders of a couple who'd just entered the pub, while Emmy started typing fast and furious again.

Emmy had confided in Finn once that she'd been suffering from writer's block after her last release, and she'd stopped by the pub to drown her sorrows. Apparently after just one hour in the pub, watching the patrons and listening to their stories, she'd been so inspired, she'd gone home and written two full chapters.

After that, she'd started bringing her laptop every day, opting to write in the pub.

Padraig had gone so far as to put a permanent "reserved" sign at her seat at the end of the bar. The only other person bestowed with that honor was Pop Pop, though his stool was in the center of the counter, right in the thick of the action, as his grandfather liked to say.

"Where's Miguel these days?" Pop Pop asked. "Don't think I've seen him around much the past few weeks."

"He's working extra hours at the precinct. Apparently, there's been a rash of robberies at some local businesses and Dad assigned the case to him."

"Good for him. I know he's trying for that promotion."

Finn nodded. "Yeah. He hopes cracking this case will give him a leg up." Finn's cell phone rang, and he showed Pop Pop the screen. "Speak of the devil. You mind if I answer this, Pop Pop?"

"Of course not."

"Hey, Miguel," Finn said, answering the phone. "What's up?"

"Did you call me, man?"

"Yeah. I'm at the pub. Wanted to invite you to join me. Can you stop by for a beer? Haven't seen you in a while."

"Damn. Wish I could, but I'm still at the precinct. Had another robbery today, and I'm buried in paperwork. Rain check?"

"Sure."

"I thought you'd be getting ready for Hunter's show tomorrow."

Finn sighed wearily. "Everything is done. Thought I'd have a quick beer and then go to bed early. Tomorrow is looking like an eighteen-hour day."

"Ouch. So...uh...LJ not available?"

"Nope. Working late."

"Ahh. So was I your first or second choice to share a beer with?"

"Be serious. You were my twelfth choice, dude," Finn said, laughing.

This wasn't the first time Miguel had made a joke about LJ replacing him in the best friend role. It felt like one of those jokes that was steeped in honesty. But Finn couldn't make himself address it because doing so would open the door to another conversation Finn wasn't ready to have. Not even with himself.

"Dick," Miguel joked, though there was no heat behind the word. "I see where I stand. You think you'd have a little sympathy. Your dad's kicking my ass around here, breathing down my neck to crack this case."

"No leads?"

"No. And it's seriously pissing me off. I'm starting to take this shit personal."

"You'll get there, Miguel. You're a great cop."

Miguel sounded tired, though grateful when he said, "Thanks, man. I needed to hear that."

"Once work settles down for both of us, we'll grab tickets to a Ravens game, okay?"

"That sounds good. Talk to you later."

"Later." Finn disconnected the call. "He's still at work," he said to Pop Pop.

"And where is your girlfriend tonight? Getting used to seeing the two of you together."

Finn grinned. "She's not my girlfriend, Pop Pop. Just a friend."

His grandfather had this sixth sense that always seemed to allow him to hear more than what was being said. "But you'd like for her to be a girlfriend?"

"I don't have time to date anyone even if I did. Fergus and I are burning the candle at both ends trying to get the security firm off the ground. I haven't had dinner before eight o'clock a single night this week."

"That didn't really answer my question, did it?"

"Pop Pop—"

Mom walked up to them before his grandfather could push the subject. "There're two of my favorite guys. Hey, Pop. Did you forget about the pumpkin pie I promised you for dessert? You still want a slice?"

Pop Pop's eyes lit up. "Well, merciful heaven, I did indeed forget. Of course, I want it."

"How about you, Finn?"

Finn shook his head. "Doesn't really go with the Guinness."

Pop Pop gave him a scandalized look. "Son, everything goes with Guinness. Now if you'll excuse me just a second, your mother never puts enough whipped cream on the pie. She's stingy."

Pop Pop hopped off the stool as Mom shook her head, chastising him. "I'd like you to taste the damn pie, Pop."

"Language, Riley."

Mom ignored him, still complaining about his disrespect for her pie as Pop Pop followed her back to the kitchen. Finn knew exactly who was going to win that argument.

Poor Mom.

Padraig came over and leaned on the counter.

If Pop Pop was king of the hopeless romantics, Padraig was the crown prince.

"So why aren't you asking Layla out?"

Finn rolled his eyes. "Emmy's talent for eavesdropping is rubbing off on you."

"He had that talent before I ever showed up," Emmy called out from her end of the counter, never looking up from the laptop.

Padraig shook his head. "Never figure out how she can listen and write at the same time. So...Layla..."

Finn took a sip of his Guinness, leaning back in his stool. "It's great to have LJ back. We have a lot of fun together. She's super easy to be around and she gets my twisted sense of humor."

"Exactly. So why aren't you asking her out on a date instead of playing the 'just friends' card? No attraction?" Padraig asked.

Finn ran his hand through his hair. "Attraction is off the charts. I want to be with her. Bad."

Padraig straightened up and refilled Emmy's wineglass, even though she hadn't asked him to. She smiled her thanks before

Padraig came back to him. "So this all feels like a no-brainer. Never known you not to go for it with a woman you like."

"It's not that simple. LJ just got out of a long relationship and she's not looking for another."

Padraig chuckled. "Didn't think that's what you were looking for either."

"She keeps saying she wants to explore her wild side. Which to her means casual hookups, one-night stands."

"Sounds right up your alley."

Finn couldn't call Padraig to task for his comment because he wasn't wrong. "I can't...I mean, with LJ, I'd want..."

"Holy shit," Padraig said when Finn couldn't finish. "You like her. You *really* like her! And you don't want to sow those wild oats with her because you're afraid she'll move on to the next guy after you're done."

Finn didn't answer. The more he thought about Layla, the more he wanted to be with her. And not just for one night. He'd never thought much about love at first sight because it sounded dumb, but something between him and Layla clicked. It was only the second time in his life he'd ever felt such a strong, instant connection.

And he wasn't letting himself consider the first time.

"I don't know what to do."

"That's simple," Padraig said. "Change her mind."

"*That's* simple?"

"You're a good guy, Finn. A catch. Just dial up the Collins charm and show Layla what she's missing out on. The fact she was in a long relationship tells me she's definitely looking for love, even if she doesn't believe it at the moment."

Finn considered that, the idea growing on him.

"And you might as well give into the dark side, cuz. The curse is real and it's found its next victim."

"Curse?" Pop Pop said, carrying a plate of whipped cream that Finn could only assume had a piece of pie underneath.

"It's not the curse," Finn said under his breath, hoping

Padraig would take the hint and change the subject. The shit-eating grin on his cousin's face proved that would not happen.

"He's got the hots for Layla, but she's not looking for a relationship," Padraig explained, dropping that bomb and then excusing himself to check on the other patrons.

Pop Pop's eyes lit up. "So you're really interested in this young woman?"

"We've only gone out a half-dozen times, Pop Pop. As friends."

"I fell in love with Grandma Sunday the first night we met. The heart is always the first to know. It takes the head a lot longer to catch up."

"She's not looking for a boyfriend."

"So...you'll convince her she is. I saw the way she looked at you the other night at dinner. She's interested too."

Pop Pop and Padraig really were a matched set. Then he considered Pop Pop's comment. "You think so?"

Pop Pop nodded. "I know so. What does Miguel think of her?"

The question caught him unaware. "Um. He hasn't met her yet."

"Really?"

"Yeah. Like I said, we've both been working a lot lately."

Pop Pop put his fork down. "But surely the two of you have talked about her. What does he think about it?"

"I haven't told him about LJ. Or, at least, not everything."

Pop Pop pierced him with a suspicious look. "What have you told him?"

"Just that my old friend, LJ, moved back to Baltimore and we've been hanging out."

"It seems to me this is the sort of thing you'd talk to your best friend about. Unless...there's something else holding you back?"

"There's nothing holding me back," he lied.

"Nothing?" It was a pointed question, and the expression on Pop Pop's face proved he knew Finn wasn't being honest.

Finn rubbed his forehead wearily. "If you have something to say, Pop Pop, you can just say it. I won't freak out."

"Of course you will. Otherwise, you would have told Miguel about this woman. But to do that would be to admit that you don't share *his* feelings for you."

Leave it to Pop Pop to be the first to so boldly say what Finn was pretty sure everyone else in his family suspected as well. He'd seen the sideways glances his cousins had given him the night of the bachelor party. If they'd noticed, it was a given the rest of the family knew because if there was one thing that didn't exist in the Collins family, it was secrets.

"Sometimes I think you're Finn in that story you used to tell me when I was a kid. The one about my namesake. Are you sure you didn't eat the Salmon of Knowledge?"

Pop Pop chuckled. "There's a difference between knowledge and just paying attention. You know that boy is in love with you, right?"

Finn winced. To hear it spoken so clearly really fucked with his current pattern of avoidance. "But I'm not gay, Pop Pop. I like women. No, I *love* women."

"I'm not entirely sure this is a question of being gay or straight. Do you love Miguel?"

Finn didn't hesitate to answer. "Of course I do. He's my best friend."

"And this Layla? You think you could love her too? And don't tell me it's only been a few weeks again. We've already covered that ground."

"I think I could. Yeah."

"I see."

Finn waited for Pop Pop to say something more, but instead, the older man picked up his fork and started eating his pie. After a few minutes, it became clear he didn't intend to say anything else.

"So...you're not going to lay any knowledge on me? No advice?"

Pop Pop smiled and patted his hand. "Only you know the truth of what's written on your heart. Until you're ready to read those words, I'm afraid you're going to be stuck in the dark. In the meantime, maybe you should head back to the kitchen and ask your mother to make you some salmon. It couldn't hurt."

## 4

Layla grinned as Finn walked into her office at the coffee shop. She was trying to pay some bills before the lunch rush started.

"Hey, gorgeous," he said, giving her a quick hug as she stood from her desk.

She tried to covertly sniff his shirt, loving the way Finn smelled...like coffee—her favorite smell on the planet—and soap. "What's up, buttercup? Haven't seen you in ages."

It had been over a week since she and Finn had gone out to dinner and had their "come to Jesus" meeting about where they both stood in their lives in terms of relationships.

"Fergus has been kicking my ass. This working-for-a-living gig sucks."

She laughed, fully aware his protest meant nothing. Finn had found his calling, and he loved what he did. He'd brought Fergus over for coffee a couple of times, and it was obvious that while they approached the business from different angles—Fergus super serious, no-nonsense, where Finn was laid-back—they were both fully committed to making it successful, especially considering the long hours they'd been putting in lately.

"Tell me about it. What do you say we both play hooky like

we did in fourth grade? Just go out for recess, then hide in the playhouse when everyone else goes back inside."

"Jesus. I'd forgotten about that. Not that we managed to steal that much extra playtime. Mrs. Arnold realized we were gone the second everyone returned to their desks and ours were empty."

"It didn't help that Landon was looking out the window nervously and tipped her off to where we were hiding."

Finn took a sip of the coffee he must have bought before coming to seek her out. "And yet he had the nerve to brag that he hadn't snitched."

"He was an amateur when it came to being bad." Layla took a sip from her own cup and winced. It had gone cold. She'd have to refill it later. Finn noticed her look and handed over his cup. She took a sip, then gave it back. They'd managed more than a few coffee breaks together over the past few weeks and realized they both liked their coffee strong enough to walk around on its own.

"Landon still is. Ever the Boy Scout. Only now he does his good deeds in a police uniform."

"Have to say, I'm not surprised by his chosen profession. Could have called that back in elementary school. Remember the day your dad came to class for Career Day? Landon followed your dad around everywhere, asking him a million questions."

Finn chuckled. "I remember. I think Dad kept hoping some of Landon's enthusiasm for his job would rub off on me. Can you imagine? Me as a cop?"

"Baltimore would never be the same."

"Listen. I'm afraid I don't have long. Just wanted to stop in and say goodbye. Fergus and I met at the office to pick up some things before heading to the airport."

"Oh crap. That's right. I forgot about your security conference."

"A whole week in Vegas, baby. I've been living for this."

Layla narrowed her eyes. "Aren't you supposed to be going to classes and learning stuff?" Layla might not know Fergus well, but she was pretty sure he was going to take the conference seriously.

Finn shrugged. "All work and no play. Want me to throw a quarter or two in the slot machine for you?"

She reached into a change jar on her desk and pulled out fifty cents. "Of course I do. I'm going to miss you. Who's going to watch the Ravens game with me Thursday night?"

She'd gotten used to having Finn around to go out for dinner or to hang out at her place, watching a movie on TV.

"Just go over to the Collins Dorm. There's always someone watching the game there. They'd love to have you join them. Especially if you take some chips and a twelve-pack of Natty Boh."

"I might just do that."

Finn stood up. "Well. I really do need to head back to the office. I'll be back in town next Monday. You have a good week."

"I will."

"And..." He paused, and Layla got the impression he was debating something with himself.

"And?" she prompted.

Finn didn't say anything more. Instead, he took a step closer and cupped her face in his hands in true Hollywood romance style—and kissed her.

Layla didn't bother to resist.

Why the hell would she? She'd been dreaming of this since the first time she'd seen him again.

She parted her lips, allowing Finn's tongue in to touch hers, then she reached for the front of his shirt, gripping it, simply for something to hold on to as Finn gave her the single hottest kiss of her life.

She'd been right. She *had* been missing out. Big-time.

Finn deepened the kiss, his hands drifting to her hair. He wrapped thick strands around his fingers and tugged, her scalp stinging, the pain translating to arousal as her nipples tightened and her pussy clenched.

Finn kissed her like his life depended on it. And Layla gave herself fully to the kiss, enjoying every stroke of his tongue and fingers and—

Finn broke the kiss, pulling away a few inches. He didn't let go of her hair. "When I get back, you and I are going to have a long talk about this wild side of yours."

"Um. Okay," she whispered stupidly.

Finn gave her another brief, hard kiss...and then he was gone.

Layla stood by her desk for a full five minutes, trying to wrap her head around that kiss and Finn's words.

Her wild side. He wanted to talk about her wild side.

What the fuck did that mean?

They'd agreed what just happened between them couldn't happen. But it did. And sweet Jesus, had it shaken her to her core. She'd been kissed in her life...by a lot of frogs.

That kiss...Finn's kiss...her head was still reeling.

Unfortunately, it changed nothing. Right?

She wasn't looking for a relationship and Finn was. The fact that his kiss had blown her socks off, and she was currently in danger of spontaneously combusting notwithstanding, she couldn't act on her more visceral needs.

Not without losing Finn as a friend.

God help her. The next week was going to take forever to pass.

But was that a good thing or a bad thing?

THE REST OF THE DAY DRAGGED, BUT THAT WAS PRETTY MUCH the standard operating procedure for Mondays. She'd intended to leave at five, but one of her employees was a no-show, while the other got sick. She hadn't been able to find anyone else to come in on such short notice, so she'd spent the last three hours working alone...on a slow night...and watching the clock. Which wasn't moving.

The last customers left, so she started cleaning up, ready to knock off a few minutes early. After all, she was the boss and she was exhausted after pulling a twelve-hour day.

Layla had just locked the front door and was halfway back to the counter, when someone walked out of the kitchen.

It took her a second to understand what she was seeing.

And when she did…panic set in.

Someone in a Pennywise mask stepped into the shop. That was scary enough. Until Layla saw the gun in his hand.

How the fuck had he gotten in? She kept the kitchen door locked.

"Keep your mouth shut and you won't get hurt." The man's deep voice was muffled slightly by the mask.

Layla struggled to catch her breath, light-headed with fear. "What do you want?"

She glanced toward the street, praying someone walking by would look in. Would see the man with the gun. Would call the cops.

Pennywise, however, was quick to take away that possibility, switching the lights off, effectively hiding what was happening inside the shop. The streetlamps outside cast shadows across the room. It wasn't pitch-black, but it was dim enough that she had to strain to see the gun-wielding clown.

He walked toward her as she steadily backed away. If she could just make it back to the door…

There was no way she could unlock it and run before he reached her.

"Please. Wait." She lifted her hands in a sign of surrender.

Layla never saw the man's hand move. Didn't realize he'd swung it upwards until the back of it landed hard on her left cheek, knocking her head back roughly enough that she saw stars.

Pain and white lights flashed behind her eyes, blinding her temporarily. Just long enough for Pennywise to grab the back of her head and shove her toward the cash register. He pushed her hard, and if he hadn't had a painful grip on her hair, she would have tripped, would have fallen.

He produced a bag and thrust it into her hands. "Open the register, bitch. Put all the money in that bag."

The task took longer than it normally would have, as her hands began trembling violently. She shoved the money in the bag, praying that was all he wanted. That he wouldn't shoot her once he'd gotten the money.

"Here," she said, handing it to him. "That's everything."

"Turn around."

Fuck. Layla was gasping for air, no breath reaching her lungs. They had seized up. Was he going to shoot her in the back? Leave her for dead.

"Please."

"Turn around!" He was leaning toward her, his horrible masked face too close, the image of the evil clown's smiling face terrifying. He raised his hand as if he might hit her again, so she spun away from him quickly.

She turned to face the wall and closed her eyes, waiting for the sound of the gun. Trying to prepare herself for the pain of the bullet ripping through her. How badly would it hurt?

Layla wasn't sure how many minutes passed before she realized she was alone, the gunman gone.

Slowly, she glanced over her shoulder. The bell above the door to the shop hadn't tinkled, so Pennywise must have escaped through the same back door, exiting to the alley.

The second she confirmed she was alone, her shaking legs gave way and she dropped to her knees on the floor, leaning forward on her hands as she fell apart, sobbing loudly, uncontrollably, her entire body quivering.

When every last tear was spent, she reached around on the counter above her until she felt her phone. Pulling it down to the floor with her—she wasn't capable of standing—she called 911.

She gave the dispatcher her name and address, grateful when

the woman continued to talk to her, to comfort her as Layla waited for the police to arrive. She said goodbye to the dispatcher when she heard the sirens and saw the flashing lights of the patrol car parking right outside the coffee shop.

Layla fought to pull herself to her feet, walking toward the front door to unlock it.

A police officer entered, gun drawn. "Did you place the call?" he asked.

"Yes."

"Is the assailant still here?"

Layla shook her head. "I think he left through the back door."

Another police car arrived, two more officers entering.

"Check the back," the first officer instructed. "Suspect left that way. How long ago did he leave?" he asked Layla.

She shrugged. She'd lost all track of time. "I—I don't know."

"See if you can catch his trail," he directed the other two. "What's your name?" the officer asked.

"Layla Moretti." She struggled to say her own name, her mouth was bone-dry, her lips suddenly chapped. Had she cried out every drop of water in her body?

"Okay, Layla. I'm Officer Garcia. Miguel. Why don't you come over here and sit down for a second?"

Layla let the kind officer guide her to one of the tables. She dropped down heavily, resting her elbows on her knees, fighting a wave of nausea as she recalled the gun pointed directly at her.

"Where are the lights?" Miguel asked.

"On the wall next to the kitchen door."

He walked behind the counter and turned on the lights. She watched him taking in the shop, studying the open cash register, glancing around for other evidence. Then he came back to her, his eyes narrowing when he saw her.

He pointed to her cheek. "What happened?"

"He hit me."

Miguel looked angry, which was strangely comforting to her.

She'd felt so alone and defenseless a few minutes earlier. Now there was someone here who cared that she'd been hurt. Even if he didn't know her from Adam.

"Do you need medical assistance? Should I call for an ambulance?"

She shook her head quickly, touching her cheek. Until Miguel pointed it out, she'd forgotten about the slap. Now she was aware of the pinpricks of pain in her cheek.

"You said *he*. It was a man who broke in? Just one?"

Layla nodded as she licked her lips. It didn't help.

Miguel seemed to understand her problem. Walking back to the counter, he reached into the refrigerator and pulled out a bottle of water.

"Here. Drink that. It'll help." He handed the water to her, then claimed the other chair at the table, pulling a notebook from his pocket.

Layla drained the entire bottle of water as Miguel waited patiently.

"Better?"

She nodded numbly. While the panic was starting to subside, it occurred to her she was suddenly very cold. "It was just one man. He came in from the back door."

"Was the door unlocked?"

"No. I never leave it unlocked."

He smiled at her. "Good for you. Was anyone else here?"

"Just me. The other guy who was scheduled to work got sick and left early."

"Can you describe the man?"

"Pennywise."

"What?" Miguel asked.

"I couldn't see his face. He was wearing a Pennywise mask."

Miguel winced. "Shit. That's one scary-ass clown."

Layla laughed, just a quick, brief bark of mirth, that prompted Miguel to smile.

"You're going to be just fine, Layla," he said.

Layla's smile faded as she clasped her freezing-cold hands together, trying to find some warmth. "He had a gun."

Miguel put down the pen he was writing with and reached his hand out to her, simply holding it open, palm up. She accepted the unspoken invitation, sliding her shaking one into his. He squeezed her hand, trying to offer her comfort. "You're safe now, Layla. He can't hurt you anymore."

She tried to let those words soak in. "I thought he was going to shoot me. Going to kill me."

Miguel's sympathetic smile and soft eyes calmed her as much as his hand gripping hers, and his next words were spoken firmly, confidently. "We're going to find the son of a bitch and he's going to pay for scaring you, for hurting you."

They sat there together in silence for a few moments, Miguel giving her time to settle her thoughts, her fears.

"I swear I'm not usually so...weak."

Miguel's grip on her hand tightened. "You aren't weak, Layla. I'd be worried about you if you *weren't* reacting this way. You just went through a very scary experience. I doubted anyone's ever pointed a loaded gun at you."

She shivered as she shook her head.

He released her hand and picked up his pen once more. "What did he say to you?"

"He gave me a bag. Told me to put all the money from the cash register in it."

"How much did he get?"

Layla shrugged. "I hadn't counted it yet, but maybe three, four hundred dollars. There isn't usually a lot of cash in the register. Most people use debit cards these days."

"Have you called the owner of the shop yet?" he asked.

"I'm the owner."

Miguel nodded. "Did the man say anything else?"

"He told me to turn around. That's when I thought he was going to shoot me. I don't know how long I stood there before I realized he was gone."

"Was there anything distinctive about his voice? An accent? A speech impediment?"

She shook her head. "No. But his voice was muffled by the mask, so... I haven't given you much to work with, have I?"

"You're doing just fine, Layla."

Before Miguel could ask any more questions, the other two officers appeared from the back.

"He broke in using a crowbar."

"You didn't hear anything?" Miguel asked her.

She shook her head. "No, but I cranked the music up pretty loud the last hour to try to keep myself awake."

The other officers walked around the counter, the larger of the two speaking. "The alley runs behind all the houses and businesses on this street, with countless outlets. He could've taken one of twenty-five possible routes. We canvassed the area. There's a shop about four doors down with a security camera in the back. If the guy went that direction, there's a chance we've got some footage of him."

Miguel nodded, sighing heavily, and Layla got a sense he wasn't holding out much hope for that. "Can you and Higson secure the back of the shop for the night?"

"Sure thing."

The two officers left them alone again.

"I'm going to need you to come down to the precinct to give a signed statement, but that can wait until tomorrow. Do you have a car outside?"

Layla shook her head. "No. My apartment is just a few blocks away. I walk to work."

She bit her lip nervously. She hadn't felt unsafe walking home any night, but now...well, she didn't like the idea of walking home tonight alone.

"I'll take you," Miguel said. "Make sure you get there safely."

"Thanks." Layla went back to the counter to retrieve her purse. The thief hadn't even thought to ask about that. She lifted it up. "He didn't ask for my money."

"He wanted to get in and out fast, and apparently he'd gotten enough."

"Enough?"

"He was probably looking for drug money."

"Oh. Yeah."

"You ready?" he asked. "The other officers will make sure the back door is secure enough for the night, until you can get someone here tomorrow to fix it. And I'll make sure someone does a drive-by every hour or so to check on the place. You might want to think about getting a security system, or at the very least, an alarm on that back door."

"I have a friend who can help me with that."

Miguel led Layla to his patrol car, opening the passenger door for her before crossing to the driver's side. She gave him directions to her apartment, the two of them riding in silence. Layla kept sneaking sideways glances at the young cop. If she had to guess, she would say he was probably about her age, though tonight, he seemed decades older than her, an adult to her trembling child.

He was biracial, with dark eyes and equally dark hair that he wore close-cropped, and he was clean-shaven. He was several inches taller than her and in great physical shape. She could see the muscles in his arms even beneath the stiff polyester of his uniform.

Layla blinked a few times, then rubbed her eyes. Exhaustion was setting in fast, yet the idea of walking into her dark apartment alone scared the hell out of her.

When they arrived, she hesitated for just a moment, looking up at the dark windows of her apartment. It was just long enough for Miguel to realize what was wrong. He opened his door, then hers.

"Come on. I'll do a quick search of your apartment for you. Make sure there aren't any monsters hiding under the bed."

She laughed. "It's not the monsters I'm worried about. It's the evil clowns."

"Completely justified fear. Those things scare the shit out of me too."

Miguel followed her upstairs, then, true to his word, he walked around her apartment as she turned on every single light in the place, checking each room and even peeking under her bed.

"All clear."

She was grateful for his kindness and feeling much safer now that he'd looked around.

He gave her his card. "There's my number if you remember anything else or if you have any questions. Don't forget to stop by the precinct tomorrow to make a statement and sign it."

"I won't."

He turned to leave, but Layla called out his name, stopping him.

"Miguel?"

"Yeah?" he said, facing her again.

She stepped toward him quickly, wrapping her arms around his waist, aware she was still shaking.

Miguel's hands landed on her waist for a moment. He was probably shocked by her impromptu hug. Then they slid around her back, embracing her as well.

"Thank you for everything." The side of her face was pressed against his brick wall of a chest, covered with Kevlar.

"You're welcome." He held her for a second longer before stepping away. He gave her a friendly, sweet smile. "You're okay, Layla. You're going to be just fine."

## 5

Miguel stood outside the coffee shop, watching as Layla wiped up a table. There were two men working behind the counter, cleaning up as well. He doubted she needed that much help in the shop on a Wednesday night, but it was obvious she was still afraid of being alone at closing time.

He walked in as she was coming to lock the front door. She heard the bell tinkle and said, "I'm sorry. We're—" She smiled when she saw Miguel, and he tried to ignore what the genuine happiness he saw reflected on her face did to him.

"Miguel! Hi."

Unfortunately, he'd been running down a couple of leads with Higson when she'd stopped by yesterday morning to sign her statement, and he had been bummed to miss seeing her again. He'd been worried about her, concerned about how she was handling the robbery. She'd obviously been very shaken up.

"Wanted to come by and check on you. Meant to stop in last night at closing time, but got called to break up a domestic dispute and by the time that was dealt with, you'd already locked up and gone home."

"That's so sweet of you."

Layla had the prettiest brown eyes Miguel had ever seen. It was the first thing he'd noticed after he'd turned on the lights in the coffee shop and gotten a good look at her. She had soulful eyes that expressed her emotions in such a way, they pulled at his heartstrings. The night of the robbery, they'd been scared, sad. Tonight, they twinkled.

He lightly brushed her cheek with the back of his finger. "Doesn't look like it bruised too badly."

She shrugged. "Foundation and concealer work magic."

Miguel was looking forward to the day they caught this bastard. He was going to make sure to exact a little extra revenge on the man for hitting Layla.

"So..." she started. "What are you up to?"

"I just got off duty."

"No uniform?"

"Changed clothes at the precinct. I'm heading home now, but wanted to check on you."

"Um. I was wondering if you'd had dinner yet."

He shook his head. "No. I worked through it. Got some left-over pizza in my fridge. Planned on reheating that in the microwave."

She pointed to the glass counter where just a few sandwiches remained. "I had half a chicken salad around four and I'm starving. Would you want to go out to eat with me? My treat. After all, you were my hero the other night. Showing up to catch the bad guy, checking for clowns under my bed."

He chuckled. "That's my job, Layla."

"I'm pretty new in town and my best friend is out of town this week. I just thought...having some company...um, might... but if you're busy..."

He grinned at her nervousness. It appeared Layla didn't usually invite men out for dates. "I'd love to grab dinner with you. But you're not paying. There's a great little place with outdoor seating by the waterfront. It's the perfect fall night— not too hot, not too cold. What do you think?"

"Sounds nice. I'd love to go there with you."

Miguel waited until her employees left, then helped her lock up the coffee shop. They crossed the sidewalk together. He stopped in front of his motorcycle. "Afraid I don't own a car, but I do have an extra helmet," he said, gesturing to the Harley. "If you don't like motorcycles, we can Uber to the restaurant."

Layla's eyes widened. "You have a motorcycle? Oh my God. Bad boy alert."

He laughed. "What?"

"I've always wanted to ride on one."

"So why haven't you?" he asked, amused by her enthusiasm.

"Because all the men in my family are crazy overprotective. If a guy had ever shown up on a Harley, they would have formed an impenetrable wall at the front door after locking me in the cellar."

Miguel was pretty sure she was joking, but... "Let's have a chat about this family of yours over dinner. I'm trying to decide whether to laugh or put you in protective custody."

She giggled. "I wish I could tell you which way to go on that, but the jury's still out on my insane family."

He lifted the extra helmet. "So I take it we're going to the restaurant on the motorcycle."

"You bet your sweet ass."

Miguel put on his helmet and climbed on, steadying the bike as Layla threw her leg over, settling on the seat behind him. He glanced over his shoulder. "Wrap your arms around my waist and hold on tight. This is going to be a fun ride."

She did as he said, her wicked grin growing wider. "That's what she said."

Miguel barked out a loud laugh as he started the bike and pulled out onto the street, loving the feel of Layla's arm circling his middle, her hands clasped together. She'd taken him at his word, holding on like her life depended on it, despite climbing on without hesitation. There was something about her that really called to him.

He was raised in the 'hood—literally—in the Bronx. His dad had been little more than a sperm donor, cutting and running before he was ever born, so it had just been him, his mom, and his uncle. He'd gotten into some trouble when he'd been younger, falling in with the wrong crowd, hanging out with gang members. If it hadn't been for his tenacious mother and his New York City cop uncle, constantly kicking his ass, he had no doubt he'd probably be in prison right now.

He pulled into the restaurant parking lot. It was late enough that the dinner rush was over, so the place was quieter than usual. As such, they were able to get a table on the large patio that overlooked the Inner Harbor.

Layla ordered a glass of wine and he asked for a beer.

"Any luck on figuring out who was in the Pennywise mask?" she asked.

He shook his head. "Unfortunately, no. We're pretty sure the guy who robbed you is the same one who's held up four other local businesses over the past few weeks. MO is basically the same. Only thing that changes is the mask. So far, in addition to the Pennywise you met, he's shown up as a white walker, Michael Myers, Trump, and an old woman."

"Guy's got a sick sense of humor. Still think it's drug related?"

"That's just one of many theories at this point. Guy robs a smaller local business, gets a few hundred bucks. It's enough for a hit or three. Then a few days later, he robs the next place. The businesses have all been within a ten-block radius, so we think he lives in the area and actually scopes out his next target prior to robbing the place."

"Are you saying he could have been a customer in my shop?"

Miguel regretted the slight tremor of fear in her voice. "Oh, Layla. Please don't worry about that. This is all a hypothesis. He also could have been standing across the street and spotted an opportunity. Everything at this point is guesswork."

"Has he hit any of the places twice?"

Miguel shook his head. "But that doesn't mean I don't think you shouldn't put an alarm in."

"Don't worry. That's definitely happening. So what you're saying is, maybe he spotted me in the shop alone close to closing time. I can assure you no one will ever work the last shift alone again."

"That's good. And yeah, he always seems to know when's the best time to strike, either right before closing time on a slow night or whenever a business is short-staffed. Plus, he manages to get away without leaving a trail. He's successfully avoiding any and all security cameras in the area, so he's either a genius or a lucky motherfucker."

Layla laughed. "Ah, the never-dull life of a cop. No luck tracing the masks?"

Miguel grinned, impressed by her question. "We've tried. Checked with local costume and Halloween shops. No one has bought all those masks at the same place. Plus, with Amazon and about a million other online shops, it's a bit like finding a needle in a haystack."

"Must be frustrating for you."

He nodded. "You have no idea. All we can do is keep going over all the evidence, tracking down leads, and hoping we can catch the guy before someone else gets robbed. Or worse."

Layla toyed with the stem of her wineglass. "I'll admit I've never been that up close and personal with a gun."

"You know, as a single woman living alone in the city, it wouldn't be a bad idea for you to consider buying a gun for protection."

"I've been thinking about that ever since the robbery."

"I teach a gun safety course once a month. At the end of it, you can apply for a concealed weapon license. I can get the information to you if you decide you're interested."

She smiled. "Thanks, Miguel. Let me think about it and I'll get back to you."

He took a sip of his beer, the two of them perusing the

menu. Miguel kept sneaking glances at Layla, distracted by her. He hadn't felt such an immediate attraction to someone since...

Fuck. Since he'd fallen head over ass in love with his straight best friend.

Miguel shoved Finn to the back of his mind, trying not to fall down that rabbit hole again. For months, he'd struggled with deciding whether or not he should talk to Finn about his feelings.

Two things kept stopping him. One, he was terrified of freaking Finn out and making things awkward between him and his best friend if Finn didn't feel the same. Of course, if it had just been that one reason, Miguel was pretty sure he would have already talked to Finn.

No, it was the second reason that stopped him from saying anything.

Miguel was ninety-nine percent sure Finn already knew how he felt. And he refused to acknowledge it, constantly putting out a pretty fucking strong "don't go there" vibe whenever Miguel felt tempted to bring it up.

Which answered the question he'd never asked.

Finn wasn't interested.

Miguel had repeated that fact over and over in his mind about a million and twelve times in the past few months, but it wasn't sinking in, wasn't sticking. Which meant Miguel had spent too many nights alone with his hand because he hadn't been able to move on, to ask someone else out.

Until Layla.

"So about this crazy family of yours..." he prompted.

Layla grinned, then told him about her papa and four older brothers. She talked about losing her mama to cancer when Layla was only in sixth grade, and he'd reached out to hold her hand as she wiped away a tear.

Then he shared about his childhood, about his mom, about how he'd always wanted siblings, about how his uncle was his idol. He told her he was bisexual, which surprised him. He'd always asserted that straight people never had to "come out" to tell others about their sexual preferences, so he didn't have to either. But there was something about Layla that had him wanting to bare his soul. She was easy to talk to, with a great sense of humor and an optimistic view of life that wasn't naïve or shaded by rose-colored glasses.

She'd been interested about his bisexuality, but there hadn't been a bit of judgment in her questions. Then she'd confessed to having a crush on another girl her freshman year in high school that ended when she and the girl shared an innocent kiss, and Layla had to admit it hadn't done anything for her. He'd cracked up when she said that, after that kiss, she was forced to live with her "straightness."

Hours passed as they ate and drank, and Miguel found himself opening up to her about things he rarely spoke of, about his troubled childhood with the gangs and his anger toward his dad for deserting him and his mom.

The waiter had to kick them out at closing time, and they'd both been surprised to discover it was so late.

They hopped back on his motorcycle and rode together in silence to her place. Miguel was certain she was holding him even tighter during this ride, and he knew it wasn't because she was afraid of falling off.

"Need me to check under your bed for the boogeyman?" he joked as he parked his bike in front of her place.

She grinned as she got off the bike and shook her head. "No. I'm okay."

Miguel hopped off his motorcycle. "I'm still going to walk you to the door."

"I appreciate that."

He locked the helmets onto his motorcycle, then took her hand as the two of them climbed the stairs to her apartment. Neither of them said anything as they walked upstairs.

"You still walking to work?" he asked. She didn't live in a

dangerous area, but he was worried about her walking alone after dark.

"Yesterday, I drove, but it meant feeding the meter all day, which was a pain. Today I was planning to grab a ride home with Seth, the guy closing up with me."

"I'm sorry you don't feel safe in the city."

She placed a hand on his arm. "You said it yourself. I'm going to be fine. Just taking me a couple of days to bounce back."

They stopped at the door as she dug into her purse for her keys.

"Well. This is me. Would you like to come in for a drink? Wine? Coffee?"

There was something about Layla that screamed innocence, even though she'd told him about her long-term boyfriend over dessert. Five years was a long time to go out with someone.

"I appreciate the offer, but it's getting late. I had a great time with you tonight."

She smiled. "Me too. You know...you could totally stop by the shop to check on me again sometime."

Miguel laughed. "I might just do that."

He wanted to kiss her. He had ever since picking her up at the coffee shop tonight. Actually, that wasn't true. He'd wanted this kiss since the night of the robbery, since she'd looked at him with those deep brown, doe-like eyes and stolen a tiny piece of his heart.

But he wasn't going to do that, wasn't going to take advantage of her when she was feeling vulnerable and scared.

Layla licked her lips and gave him a shy smile. Then she lifted her face to him.

Damn. She was the definition of temptation.

"Layla," he started, moving the tiniest bit closer to her.

His phone vibrated loudly. He'd turned off the ringer during dinner, but technically—until the robbery case was solved—he was on call. It was his case.

"Shit." He stepped back and gave her an apologetic look.

"Sorry. I need to…" He glanced at the screen and saw Higson's number. "I have to take this."

He answered, not surprised when the other officer said, "Someone in a Darth Vader mask just robbed a convenience store on the corner of Doyle and Bank. Shots were fired this time."

"I'll be right there." Miguel hung up. "I need to go. I had a great time tonight."

"So did I."

Miguel started to walk away, then turned back to her. "I'm going to call you tomorrow."

She laughed. "I'd like that. A lot."

Miguel waved as he said goodbye.

As he hustled down to his motorcycle, he realized Layla had done the impossible.

Made him forget about Finn for just a few short hours.

Progress.

$$\text{\ding{107}} \quad 6 \quad \text{\ding{106}}$$

Layla wiped a table with way more aggression than was necessary. She was feeling decidedly bitchy today, something that was obvious, given the wide berth her employees were giving her. She'd managed to snap at both of them several times over small shit, and if she weren't in such a sour mood, she'd feel guilty for that.

As it was, her mood only got progressively darker as the day wore on.

She had seen Miguel once more since they'd gone out to dinner. They'd shared a quick lunch break at a deli down the street on Thursday. He hadn't kissed her, but she'd wanted him to.

Or at least, she did until she thought about Finn. Then she didn't know what the hell she wanted.

Lately it felt like Murphy's Law was guiding every flipping minute of her life. She had invited Miguel to her place for dinner on Friday, but then her oldest brother, Tony, had shown up Friday morning for a surprise visit. Layla chose to call it a sneak attack.

She'd begrudgingly canceled with Miguel, not willing to put the hot cop in front of the firing squad—AKA, her family—so soon. A lifetime with the Moretti boys had taught her how to play the game better, and rule one with her brothers was, "keep them in the dark for as long as possible."

Tony, the asshole, had remained all weekend, not leaving until Sunday evening. She'd called to invite Miguel over for pizza, but he'd been on duty. The only thing that had appeased her slightly was the fact Miguel had sounded like he was as disappointed as she was.

She'd texted back and forth with Finn throughout the week as well, but she hadn't mentioned the robbery or Miguel, wanting to talk to him about both in person.

She knew Finn well enough to know he would freak out if she told him about Pennywise and the gun, and she didn't want to ruin his trip to Vegas. He'd been looking forward to it.

She also wasn't sure exactly how he'd feel about Miguel. Finn had thrown her for a loop with that kiss. He'd mentioned wanting to talk to her about exploring her wild side before leaving, and she was pretty damn sure she knew what that meant. What she couldn't figure out was what her answer should be.

Layla had anticipated having this week alone to sort it all out in her mind, but then Pennywise had shown up, scared the fuck out of her and then tossed Miguel into her life.

Now she was more confused than ever. And it didn't help that her dreams had gotten decidedly kinkier this week as she'd begun alternating between Miguel and Finn as the hero in her fantasies. Both men had ignited some pretty powerful desires inside her, and her vibrator was getting one hell of a workout.

Something had to give. And soon.

Masturbation was one thing, but the lack of real sex was starting to get to her.

But...achieving that goal was harder than she'd expected.

Finn was her friend and she knew he wanted a relationship, something she couldn't give him. Even though she wanted to expand on that kiss of his more than she cared to admit.

And then there was Miguel. They'd only known each other a

week, but it felt like longer. She'd felt an instant connection to him...an instant attraction.

God. Maybe she should have just stuck it out with Marco. Because she sucked at playing the field.

She tossed the dirty rag she'd been wiping the tables with into a tub of soapy water in the sink. "I'm going to do some paperwork in my office for a little while." She ignored the audible sighs of relief both employees released as she walked away from them.

Her eyes started to go fuzzy when she was still working on her computer two hours later, trying to finalize next week's order. She rubbed them wearily. Layla shut the computer off, ready to kick off early.

She'd go home and have a nap.

She huffed a short breath and admitted the truth. She was going home to play with her vibrator.

Then she'd take the nap.

"Hey, stranger."

She glanced toward the door excitedly at the sound of Finn's voice. She raced around her desk and hugged him. "You're home!"

Finn returned her embrace, keeping his arms wrapped around her for a solid minute. Then he pulled away slightly, his hands still resting on her waist. "I might go out and come back in again. That was a damn good welcome home."

She laughed. "I missed you, you lunatic. Did I win any money in the slot machine?"

He shook his head. "Nope. I'm afraid not. Fergus and I discovered we're pretty shit gamblers."

"How was the conference?"

She stepped back to her desk, leaning against it as Finn sat in one of the chairs in front of it. "Good. Informational."

"Does that mean you went to all the sessions like a good boy?"

He chuckled tiredly. "Fergus is a pain in the ass when it comes to shit like that. Always was a good student."

"While you daydreamed and played hooky?"

"I'll have you know I was a solid C student. Didn't fail. Just didn't..."

"Work too hard," she finished for him.

He grinned. "I have to admit it's different when it's your career you're learning about. Heard some great presentations about hand-to-hand combat and learned about the latest in security systems."

"Speaking of which," she said, taking the opening he'd just provided. "I know you and Fergus provide services to larger corporations, rather than personal security, but I was wondering if you'd be able to help me put an alarm system in here at the shop."

"Of course I will. Saw some really state-of-the-art stuff at the conference."

"Good, because..." she paused.

"Because?"

"Well. There was sort of an incident here last Monday night."

Finn's eyes narrowed. "An incident?"

"The store was robbed."

"What?" Finn stood up. "When? How?"

"I was closing up and a guy broke in through the back kitchen door."

"Jesus." Finn ran his hand through his hair. "Were you alone?"

Layla nodded. "Yeah. He had a gun and—"

"A gun?!"

Yep. She'd known Finn wouldn't take the news about the robbery well. He started cursing.

"Why in the hell didn't you call me? Tell me about this?"

"You were in Vegas."

"So?"

"It's okay, Finn. He just asked for the money, I gave it to him, then he left. I called the cops and that was it."

"What did the guy look like?"

"Pennywise."

"The clown?"

She nodded. "He was wearing a mask."

"We texted all week, LJ. Why would you keep this from me?"

"I didn't want you to worry. I wanted you to enjoy your trip and the conference. Like I said, I'm fine."

He studied her face, and she winked, trying to prove to him she really was okay.

"Don't do that again," he said, his hands cupping the sides of her face.

"What? Wink?"

"Leave me in the dark. We're friends, LJ, and I care about you. The fact that someone held a gun on you scares the fuck out of me. I don't care where I am or what time it is. Anything else like that ever happens to you, you call me. Got it?"

"Got it."

"Promise?" he added.

"Promise."

Her insides heated and turned to goo over Finn's concern. If she'd told her brothers about the robbery—which she hadn't because she wasn't insane—they would have flipped out as well, and they probably would have demanded the same from her.

And while she would have given that promise to her brothers begrudgingly, grumbling about their overprotectiveness, granting Finn the same vow didn't bother her at all. Instead, it made her feel safe, cared for...horny.

Okay, Jesus. Everything made her horny these days.

Finn grasped her hand. "Show me the door he broke into."

She led him to the kitchen, showing him the newly repaired door. She'd had the repairman replace it with a steel door and add an extra dead bolt. It was probably overkill, but it made her feel better.

Finn borrowed a tape measure, writing things down on a piece of paper she provided. "I'm going to go back to the office and start pricing out some alarm systems. I think we need to put surveillance cameras on both doors as well. That can be a pretty good deterrent by itself."

"Okay. Listen, I was hoping we could talk about that other thing you said…just before you left last week."

Finn didn't hear her, clearly distracted, still looking around the kitchen, then walking back to the front door. "You're lucky you weren't hurt," he murmured. "A fucking gun."

She wanted to talk to Finn about Miguel, and about Finn's desire to discuss her wild side, but it was obvious the timing was wrong. He was measuring the large front window, still recording everything, still muttering about the danger she'd been in.

Finally, he folded the paper and put it in his back pocket. "Did they catch the guy?" he asked.

She shook her head. "No. Not yet."

He scowled, his eyes dark. "I'm going to call my dad. See if they have any leads."

"You don't have to do that," she said. She started to tell him that she was still in touch with Miguel, and she knew exactly what the police knew, but Finn didn't give her a chance.

"I'm going to start working on this today. Top priority."

"Finn," she said, "listen. I'm fine. Really. I was hop—"

Finn pulled her toward him, hugging her hard. "Have dinner with me tonight."

It wasn't a question, but it wasn't like she was going to turn him down anyway. She'd missed him and she wanted to talk to him.

"Okay."

He placed a sweet kiss on her forehead. "Meet me at the pub at six?"

She nodded. "Sure."

For the first time since she'd told him about Pennywise and the gun, he smiled. "I missed you so much."

"Ditto."

Finn left, and Layla grabbed her purse as she left instructions for her employees and headed home.

She didn't bother to stop moving as she entered her apartment, slowly stripping on her way to the bedroom. Her purse was dumped by the door, her jacket a few feet from that. Then she paused to kick her shoes off at the beginning of the hallway. Her shirt was tossed down just outside the bedroom, her bra falling right beside it. Her jeans were shed at the bedroom door, her panties by the bed.

She was a regular erotic Gretel, leaving a trail of clothing breadcrumbs straight to her bedroom. If only there was someone coming along behind her to follow the path.

She reached for the vibrator in her nightstand drawer, then sank down on the mattress, lying on her back to stare at the ceiling for a moment.

Closing her eyes, she pictured Finn's face, his sweet smile, the concern in his voice earlier. It was nice and helped her relax. Then her thoughts drifted back to Finn's joke that he would ruin her for all other men, and she let herself imagine exactly how he would do that...

*"Good girl," Finn murmured from the doorway of her bedroom.*

*"You told me to wait for you here," she said, smiling softly as she added the word, "naked."*

*Finn walked over to the bed, pulling his shirt over his head as he did so. She licked her lips as he and his six-pack abs knelt one knee on the mattress next to her. "Are you wet for me?" he asked.*

*"Yes," she whispered.*

*"Show me."*

*Layla's fingers slid along her slit, the moisture from her body coating them. She lifted them to show Finn.*

*"Suck off the juices for me, LJ. Show me exactly how you'd suck my cock."*

*Her fingers shook slightly—not from fear, but from need—as she placed two of them at her mouth without putting them in. She painted her lips with her arousal, loving the groan of desire Finn gave her.*

*"You're a dirty girl," he said, drawing one fingertip over her chest, over her breast, before teasing her nipple. "Use your free hand to cup your tit."*

*She did exactly as he said, loving the way he commanded her, knowing all the ways to turn her on.*

*"Now squeeze it. Hard."*

*Layla squeezed, gasping at how good it felt to touch herself this way.*

*"Pinch your nipple while you suck on those fingers."*

*She slipped her fingers into her mouth, the tanginess of her body's juices coating her tongue. She sucked hard on them as she applied pressure to her nipple, her hips rising from the mattress as she sought some much-needed stimulation between her legs.*

*"Touch me," she pleaded with him.*

*"Not yet," he said. "You're not ready."*

*"I am," she insisted. "God. I am!"*

*Finn picked up her vibrator and handed it to her. "I haven't gotten my show yet. You're going to fuck yourself with this, let me see how pretty you are when you come. I want to watch your pussy clench down on that toy and know that soon, it's going to be my dick you're squeezing like a vise."*

*Layla's breath was stilted, and it was hard to get air to her lungs. She wanted him, needed him.*

*She slowly slid the vibrator inside, stroking it in and out shallowly a few times as her arousal covered it, making it slide in easier, deeper on each thrust.*

*Once it was fully lodged, she held it there, her eyes finding his.*

*"Turn it on, LJ. On high."*

*"I won't be able to stop myself from coming."*

*He gave her a sweet smile. "I didn't ask you to stop. I asked you to show it to me."*

*"Fuck," she breathed as she switched the toy on high. Her back arched*

*as the first powerful pulses rumbled through her body. "God!" she cried out, her eyes drifting closed.*

*She pumped the toy in and out roughly.*

*"That's it," Finn muttered, his lips next to her ear, his breath hot on her cheek. "Fuck yourself with it. Harder, Layla."*

*Her eyes still closed, she moved the vibrator faster, driving it deeper as the pulsing toy stroked every sensitive hotspot inside her.*

*"Find your G-spot," Finn demanded. "Stroke it with the vibrator."*

*She felt his strong, large hand on hers, pressing the toy against that magical spot, working it in deeper than she'd ever dared to do on her own.*

*White lights flashed behind her shut eyelids as her pussy began to tingle with that first telltale sign that her orgasm was close.*

*"Oh my God." Her voice was breathless, husky.*

*She bent her knees, her feet flat on the mattress as she lifted herself up on every downstroke of the vibrator. "Fuck. Fuck me. God. Finn!"*

*As her orgasm struck, Finn kissed her, soaking up the sound of her screams.*

*He didn't release her until her climax began to subside.*

*"Open your eyes, LJ. Open your eyes and look at us."*

*Us?*

*She opened her eyes to find Finn lying next to her, while Miguel knelt between her legs, her dripping vibrator in his hands.*

LAYLA BOLTED UPRIGHT, HER EYES FLYING OPEN AS SHE dropped her vibrator. Her body still rumbled from her orgasm.

Holy masturbation masterpiece.

It took several minutes for her to land, for her to come to grips with her fantasy.

It had felt so real.

So fucking real.

And it was *that* fact that had her crashing to earth. Because it wasn't just Finn trying to ruin her for other men. It was Miguel too.

## ❧ 7 ❧

Finn had grabbed a corner booth at the pub, settling in to wait impatiently for Layla to arrive. He'd missed her like crazy this past week, and he'd intended to initiate his plan to woo her this afternoon in her office. That plan had been effectively blown out of the water when Layla told him about the robbery.

At that point, he'd briefly lost his mind as true terror kicked in when he considered all the things that could have happened to her while he was on the other side of the country.

It was bad enough to think about a man holding a gun on her and stealing her money, but Finn's imagination had led him down darker paths all afternoon when he considered how much worse things could have been. It didn't help that he was back in Baltimore, fresh from a session at the conference that detailed some horrifying real-life attacks and how steps could have been taken to prevent them.

Layla could have been raped or killed.

He closed his eyes and—for the hundredth time today—tried to shut those thoughts down.

Then he glanced at the brochures he'd brought from the

office to show her over dinner. He had narrowed her security system options down to three. His only criteria for the systems had been that he had to feel safe leaving her alone in the shop with them. As such, her coffee shop was about to become Fort Knox in terms of security.

He'd left the office late and hadn't had a chance to call his dad to see if the police had any leads on the robbery, so he made a mental note to do that first thing in the morning.

Actually, he'd call Miguel to ask. He wanted to touch base with him. Neither of them had texted over the past week, and it occurred to Finn this was the longest he'd gone without talking to or seeing his best friend, and he was a little bit worried about why they'd gone radio silence.

*He* hadn't texted because he knew he couldn't keep lying to Miguel about Layla and what she meant to him. The two of them had a day of reckoning coming...very soon.

But he wasn't sure why Miguel had stopped texting, and that's what was really bothering him.

"Hey, good-looking."

He looked up and smiled as Layla slid into the booth next to him.

"Been waiting long?" she asked.

He shook his head. "Only been here long enough to order myself a Guinness and you a glass of wine."

As if on cue, Padraig came over to deliver the drinks. "Hello, Layla," his cousin said. "It's about time you made your way back to the pub. Thought I was going to have to go out looking for you."

Layla laughed, and she and Padraig shared a few pleasantries before he returned to the bar.

His cousin Yvonne popped over with menus. "Sorry it took me a minute to get over here. We're short-staffed tonight."

"No problem. LJ only just got here."

Like Padraig, Yvonne hung out a couple of minutes, chatting. "By the way, the rest of my stuff will be out this weekend," she said. Yvonne had been slowly moving all of her things out of the Collins Dorm and over to her boyfriend Leo's house. "Just in time for Oliver and Gavin to move in."

"Oliver, the baby cousin, is moving in?" Layla asked.

Yvonne laughed, as Finn said, "I guess it's time for us to stop referring to Ollie as the baby. He's been old enough to legally drink for a year now."

Oliver, the youngest of Finn's cousins, had been chomping at the bit to move into the apartment above the pub for a year now. He and his best friend/foster brother, Gavin, had been working construction with Oliver's dad, Sean, and their uncles, Justin and Killian, since graduating from high school.

Aunt Lauren had been very resistant about the idea of "her boys" flying the coop, unable or unwilling to do the empty nest thing, and because Oliver had a heart as big as New York City, he'd appeased her until Sean was able to convince her the boys were getting too damn old to live at home.

With Yvonne moving out, the timing was perfect for Oliver and Gavin to move in, and Finn was looking forward to having a bunch of cousins living in the apartment again. With just him, Colm and Darcy left in the dorm, it had been getting kind of quiet lately.

"Well, I better get back to work. I'll take your orders in a few minutes." With that, Yvonne went to check on other tables.

Finn picked up the brochures he'd brought from work and handed them to Layla. "I want you to take a look at these three security systems. They're the best."

For a few minutes, he went over the pros and cons of the systems, answering her questions. He could tell from her countless number of questions she was still pretty shaken up from the robbery, though she was trying to put on a good face.

Finn wrapped his arm around the back of the booth once she tucked the brochures in her purse, moving closer to her. "I didn't get a chance to call my dad to see if they've caught the guy."

Layla took a sip of her wine. "You don't have to call. I know they haven't caught him yet. I've..." She paused for just a second, but long enough to catch Finn's attention. "I've been in contact with the cop who answered the call the night of the robbery."

"Oh?" Finn's Spidey senses went on alert.

"Yeah. We, um, we've actually gone out a couple of times... just dinner once and a lunch."

Finn had been prepared to lay it on the line for Layla tonight, ready to pick up the conversation they'd started in the Italian restaurant. He'd let her convince him that they couldn't sleep together, couldn't risk their friendship.

But he couldn't let go of the feeling that they would be pretty perfect together. He simply wanted a chance to prove that to her. To tell her he wanted to be her wild-side guy.

Unfortunately, the jealousy that reared its ugly head when she mentioned going on a date with someone else only proved just how far gone he already was when it came to Layla.

"Did you kiss him?"

"No, but..."

Layla frowned, and he could tell he'd fucked up with his first question. He needed to dial his jealousy back a notch or twenty. She wasn't his girlfriend, and she'd been nothing but honest with him in terms of her intentions, her desire to play the field.

"Finn," she started.

"No? Did you want to kiss him?" he asked, aiming for light-hearted.

Her eyes narrowed, and he could tell he wasn't fooling her.

"I don't think—"

Finn didn't give her a chance to call him out. Instead, he did the only thing his jealous, aroused, fucked-up head could think to do. He pulled her toward him and kissed her.

There was nothing gentle about the kiss. He took her lips like the goddamn plane was going down, like he was headed off to war, like—

"Finn?"

He and Layla pulled apart as Finn turned toward the sound of Miguel's voice.

Only Miguel wasn't looking at him. He was looking at...

"Layla?"

Confused, Finn glanced from Miguel to Layla. "You know LJ?" he asked.

"*LJ?*"

Fuck. There was no mistaking the angry tone in Miguel's voice.

"Miguel is the cop I was telling you about," Layla said. She looked back at Miguel and forced a smile, though it was clear she was uncomfortable. "LJ stands for Layla Jean," she explained. "I was named after both my grandmothers."

"I was named after a soap opera character," Miguel said, though the words came out wooden.

"How do you guys know each other?" Layla asked.

"Miguel is," Finn paused, "my best friend."

"Oh. I didn't realize you knew each other."

Finn watched her cheeks flush and he could tell she didn't know what else to say. How could she? Her dating experience was limited to one guy.

Miguel's scowl darkened, his gaze drilling straight through Finn. "It's clear I've interrupted something. I'll leave you two to your...date."

Before Finn could say anything, Miguel turned, storming toward the exit.

"I'm sorry," Layla said quickly. "I don't know..."

Her words faded away.

She didn't have a clue what was going on, but she was astute enough to see just how badly that scene had gone.

"You have nothing to apologize for. You didn't do anything wrong." Finn didn't have time to explain anything to her at the moment. Hell, he didn't know *how* to explain it. "Can you give me a minute, LJ? I need to tell Miguel something."

"Sure," she said, as Finn slid out of the booth and hurried to the door. He expected Miguel would be halfway to the parking lot by now, so he was surprised to find him standing on the sidewalk just outside the pub.

"Miguel," Finn said, drawing his friend's attention.

Miguel spun around angrily. "What?"

Finn wasn't sure what to say. Layla said she'd gone out with Miguel a couple times, but they hadn't kissed. Finn tried to recall the last time his friend had even gone on a date. It had been a while.

Since before the bachelor party in June.

"Can we talk about this?" It was a weak start, but he was scrambling here.

"Are you interested in her?" Miguel asked.

Finn nodded. "Yeah. Are you?"

"What if I am?" Miguel asked. "Are you going to step aside?"

Finn hesitated, then shook his head. "I like her, Miguel. I like her a lot."

"Why did you let me think LJ was a man?"

Miguel's question hit him like a punch to the gut. Finn didn't have an answer. At least not one he wanted to say aloud. In truth, there were too many reasons. He'd seen Miguel's jealousy every time Finn mentioned going out on a date.

Plus, he was afraid if he told Miguel about his feelings for Layla, it might...fuck...it might force his friend's hand about admitting his own.

The silence lingered for too long.

"I guess that's my answer."

Finn frowned. "What's that supposed to mean?"

Miguel pointed an angry finger at him. "Don't. Don't pretend you don't know. I don't deserve that."

Finn's heart raced as his chest constricted, and he was overcome with guilt. His friend was right. He *didn't* deserve it. He didn't deserve any of this. "Miguel—" he started, but his throat closed up and his voice failed him.

"I'm done pretending this doesn't exist, Finn."

Finn sucked in a deep breath, searching for an answer.

Miguel never gave him the chance. "Fuck it."

He strode right up to Finn and kissed him. Hard.

Finn stood stock-still for a hot minute...before his lips softened and he gripped Miguel's hips, pulling his best friend closer as he kissed him back.

Finn didn't have a clue how long they stood there, lips locked together. It could have been mere seconds or hours. Finn had kissed at least a hundred girls in his life, but this...Jesus... this was unlike anything he'd ever experienced. Miguel was gripping the back of Finn's neck firmly, unwilling to let him pull away.

Not that Finn was trying to. Their lips were smashed together hard, their tongues touching, the taste of the Guinness Finn had just been drinking blending with Miguel's flavor —coffee.

Miguel's other hand wrapped around Finn, gripping his ass, pulling him forward to make certain Finn felt his erection, ensuring Miguel felt his.

Finn was hard. Rock-hard.

When they pulled apart, they were both panting, gasping, staring at each other.

A soft intake of breath drew their attention to the door of the pub, where Layla stood.

"LJ," Finn whispered.

Jesus Christ. He'd fucked up *everything* tonight.

Layla took a step closer, then another. "That was...the single hottest thing I've ever seen in my life."

Miguel chuckled, though there wasn't much humor in the sound. "I'm so sorry, Layla. I really screwed up tonight. I should go home—"

"Wait!" Layla reached out, placing her hand on Miguel's arm to stop him from running again. "You're not screwing anything up. I just didn't realize the two of you—"

"We're not," Finn and Miguel said in unison.

"But…" Layla was clearly confused. She studied their faces for a moment before asking, "That was your first kiss?"

Miguel nodded.

Then she looked at Finn, who was barely holding it together.

"Your first kiss with a man?"

Finn tried to clear his throat to answer, but when the lump wouldn't budge, he was forced to merely nod as well.

"Then you should do it again," she whispered to them.

Finn shook his head. "It's not that simple, LJ."

She smiled at them. "Of course it is. It's the simplest…" She kissed Miguel, a soft, sexy kiss that lasted seconds but packed a punch, as far as Finn was concerned. When they broke apart, Layla finished her sentence "…thing in the world."

The image of Layla and Miguel kissing was as hot as the kiss his best friend had just planted on *him*.

She turned toward Finn then, gripping his waist as she moved into his personal space. "It's as simple as…" This time, *he* was rewarded with the kiss. Her lips parted, allowing his tongue to swipe in for a taste. He lifted his hands to her face, deepening the kiss. She pulled back only a millimeter to finish her comparison. "…breathing," she whispered, her own breath hot on his face.

She took a step back and looked at them expectedly. "Your turn," she prompted.

Finn felt frozen in place, a huge, shapeless chunk of ice. Confused-as-fuck ice. And Miguel didn't look any better.

When neither of them moved, Layla sighed. "I'm sorry. I shouldn't have pushed you. I think I'm the one who should leave. Give the two of you some space."

"No," Finn said quickly, grasping her arm, feeling Miguel's gaze on his face. He couldn't look at Miguel, couldn't move.

Layla tried to move his hand from her arm. "Finn. I think it would be for the best if I—"

"Went home with us," Miguel interjected.

Finn and Layla both turned to look at Miguel, and it

occurred to Finn that his best friend was reeling too. In this, they were both lost souls.

"What?" Finn asked.

Miguel looked at Finn, then Layla. "I think the three of us should sleep together."

❦   8   ❦

Miguel stared at Layla hard, for a full thirty seconds, praying she wouldn't throw a punch, wouldn't knee him in the nuts for his outrageous suggestion.

He'd seen the way Finn had looked at Layla and he'd known. Known in an instant that his friend was falling hard and fast for the woman.

That fact might have been harder to take if Miguel hadn't gotten to know her, hadn't felt an undeniable attraction to her as well.

Layla returned his gaze, and he watched a myriad of emotions cross her face. Then he saw the one that had set his heart racing, that stole all the air from his lungs.

He saw understanding. She nodded just once, the slightest dip of her head. He was sure Finn hadn't seen it. But he had.

"What?" Finn asked again.

Miguel repeated his assertion. "I think the three of us should go back to my place together."

"I agree," Layla said, the strength in her voice prompted Miguel to grin.

The attraction he'd felt to her the night they'd gone out to dinner was a mere flicker to his feelings now. She was incredible.

"What the hell are you saying, LJ?" Finn, however, was still struggling.

Layla, God bless her, found the perfect way to explain Miguel's suggestion. "It's obvious you two have feelings for each other, but you're not sure how to start. Think about it. A three-some solves all our problems. The two of you get to expand on this thing between you, and I get to explore my wild side. The perfect night. For all of us."

Miguel wasn't a hundred percent sure this was the right thing to do, but he didn't have any of the answers when it came to Finn. Then, he'd taken one look at Layla and found a way. Finn wanted her. Hell, Miguel wanted her.

He'd been searching for a way to convince Finn to see him, not as a best bud, but as a man he could love—emotionally and physically.

Miguel had never fallen for a straight man...not until Finn. So he was pretty much clueless about how to seduce a guy who wasn't ready to admit he wanted to take a male lover.

"Wild side?" Miguel asked, hoping to dispel some of the tension surrounding them.

"I told you about the guy I'd been dating, the one I recently broke up with?" Layla asked.

Miguel nodded. Past relationships had been one of the million things they'd talked about the night at the restaurant. At the time, he'd hoped they'd have at least two dozen more dates.

Jesus.

What a night. To find out the guy he was in love with was falling for the same girl *he* was sucked. There wasn't enough liquor in the world to drown out these fucked-up sorrows. "I remember. Marco, right?"

"Well, he was actually the only guy I've ever dated. And by dated, I mean slept with."

"You've only been with one guy?" Miguel wasn't sure why that surprised him so much. It was probably because he had a hard time believing any man who met her wouldn't want to be with her. She was beautiful and funny and the coolest woman he'd ever met—including Finn's sisters and female cousins, who were fucking awesome.

"Yep. Marco, Mr. Missionary, was it."

Miguel laughed at her less-than-amused tone.

"And she's determined to explore her wild side," Finn continued. "Meaning casual sex."

"And one-night stands," Layla added with an adorable grin. "Preferably with two hot guys who kiss each other too."

Layla was clearly serious about accepting his offer, but there was something in the tone of Finn's voice that set off an alarm. Miguel had never known Finn to date a woman for very long at all. Instead, he preferred to keep his relationships simple, the no-strings-attached variety. He'd confided in Miguel once that he wasn't ready to settle down, and he didn't see himself being ready until he was at least thirty-five. Miguel had laughed and given him shit for putting an age limit on it, but Finn had insisted he was serious, and he'd believed him.

"The two of you have been going out quite a bit lately," Miguel said, his eyes locked on Finn's. "You haven't..."

Finn shook his head. "We're friends. We didn't want to mess that up."

That was the biggest line of bullshit his friend had ever uttered, and Miguel called it out with a disbelieving snort.

Finn narrowed his eyes, but not in anger. It looked the tiniest bit like fear. Finn had fallen for Layla, that much was obvious. What was also becoming clear was Finn hadn't told Layla.

Fuck. His stomach clenched.

Had Miguel waited too long to make his move?

With both of them.

Suddenly, he wasn't so sure he was right to push the threesome idea. How could he step between his best friend and the woman he loved?

"I should go," Miguel said, when that thought turned his insides to ice. He turned to walk away.

"No."

If it had been Layla who'd uttered that word, Miguel would have persisted, would have bowed out, made his excuses and kept walking. Finn was his best friend, and he wouldn't screw up his chance at something real with Layla, despite Miguel's feelings.

But it wasn't Layla who'd stopped him.

It was Finn.

Miguel shifted, facing Finn. "No?"

Before Finn could explain, Layla reached for both of their hands. "Please," she said. "Please don't overthink this or make excuses why we shouldn't do it. Unless..." She studied Finn's face. "Unless I'm a third wheel and in the way." Layla's voice trembled slightly.

Miguel didn't like that, didn't ever want her to think she wasn't wanted. Pretty obviously by both he *and* Finn.

But Finn was the first to speak. "I want to be with you so bad it hurts, LJ. I have since the first day I ran into you at the coffee shop."

"Oh." She smiled sweetly. "Yeah, that kiss you gave me was kind of a tip-off."

Finn chuckled for just a moment, the mirth gone when Layla turned to Miguel.

"Miguel? Does the offer still stand?" she asked quietly.

Miguel wasn't sure if his next words were the smartest or the dumbest he'd ever uttered, but he didn't hold back. "It does."

Finn turned to him, scowling. "Jesus, Miguel. Why don't we take a few seconds and talk about this? This isn't the sort of thing you just jump into."

"Actually, we've had months to have this talk. We haven't. So fuck it. Layla is right. This feels *exactly* like the sort of thing you have to jump into." Miguel reached for Layla's hand. "Thinking too much is why we're in this position to begin with. Besides, I want Layla...every bit as bad as you."

Layla grinned, a combination of shock and delight. "Really?"

Miguel rolled his eyes, amazed that she obviously had no clue how beautiful she was. "Of course I do. I just didn't feel right taking advantage of you. You were scared after that break-in and—"

Layla cut him off. "You're not taking advantage. I don't know how to explain it, but watching the two of you kiss just now…"

Miguel smiled, then turned to his best friend. He saw a light of understanding dawn in Finn's eyes, and he realized his friend got it. Completely. He'd been just as blown away watching Layla kiss Miguel.

As soon as he realized that, Miguel knew without a doubt that this idea was the answer to a prayer.

And then, because he was terrified of Finn coming to his senses or finding some argument against this, Miguel started tugging Layla toward the parking lot. "Are you coming, Finn?"

Finn stood motionless for no more than three beats of Miguel's heart, then he raced to catch up with them. He was relieved when his friend didn't try to continue the argument. Instead, he reached for Layla's other hand and said, "I hope to hell the two of you know what you're doing."

Layla led them to her car since Miguel only had the bike and Finn's car keys were up in his apartment. "Drive to my place," Miguel said, as he climbed into the passenger seat and gave her directions. He'd seen Layla's bed, and it wasn't big enough for what they planned to do. Miguel's king-size one would do the trick.

None of them spoke as Layla drove to Miguel's apartment, the sexual tension in the car thick enough to cut with a knife.

Once they arrived, Miguel led them to the living room, thinking perhaps they should start slowly. He'd been called a wild child by his mother and uncle since birth, and he'd owned it. The idea of having a threesome with Layla and Finn definitely spoke to that adventurous side of him.

Layla was less nervous now than she'd been outside the pub. In fact, she was starting to look downright excited.

She pulled her purse off and tossed it to the coffee table.

Unable to resist expanding on that first, too-brief kiss, Miguel reached for her.

Pulling her close, he bent his head to steal another kiss. She'd initiated the one outside the pub, and he'd let her lead. He couldn't do that this time. Cupping her cheeks with his hands, he deepened the connection, his tongue darting out to stroke her lower lip.

"Open your mouth," he whispered.

Layla's tongue met his, her hands gripping his waist tightly.

Miguel was hyperaware of Finn, so he knew his friend had moved to stand directly behind Layla. But that was all he saw before he closed his eyes and gave himself up to the kiss. Layla mewed—almost desperately—when his hands left her face and traveled along her shoulders.

So much for taking it slow. All Miguel could think of was dragging her to the floor and sliding into her wet heat.

His hands moved lower, seeking out her breasts.

But when he got there...

Miguel stepped away and opened his eyes, just in time to see Finn's hands leave Layla's breasts. His friend had been stroking them, toying with them as they kissed.

Jesus. Miguel was going to have to keep his eyes open because he refused to miss a minute of any of this.

Layla graced them with an understanding smile. He and Finn had both released her the moment their hands had touched. There was going to be a steep learning curve tonight.

"Maybe we should start slower. Do you have anything to drink?" she asked.

Miguel nodded. "Yeah. Sorry. I should have offered instead of—"

"Don't ever apologize for leading with a kiss. That was totally hot."

He grinned. "I think there's some beer in the fridge. I'll get it."

"Nope. I will," Layla said. "Just point me in the right direction."

"It's through there, but—" Miguel said, pointing to a doorway. Layla was gone before he could insist on going. He started after her. "I should help her find some glasses."

Finn reached out and put a hand on Miguel's arm to stop him. His first intentional touch since they'd shared the kiss. "No. She's giving us a second to get our shit together. I think we should take it."

Miguel hadn't considered that, but he realized Finn was probably right. "Okay."

"I don't know what you intend to have happen tonight." Finn spoke in hushed tones. "But LJ...she's only ever been with one guy, Miguel."

"I know."

"Are you serious about going through with this?"

Miguel nodded. "I can't tell you how much I want this."

Finn gave him a crooked, somewhat rueful smile. "Fuck, man. Me too. But..."

Miguel knew what part was holding Finn back, and he decided to let his friend off the hook. For now. "Tonight is for her, Finn. She wants to go wild. We'll give her that."

Finn considered his offer. "Are you sure?"

"Yeah. I am." He was. In all honesty, that was about the only damn thing Miguel was sure of tonight.

Finn studied his face. "We're going to talk about that kiss, Miguel. I swear to God we are. But not tonight. Is that okay?"

Miguel felt some of the weight that had been pressing down on his chest lift. Finn's easy smile was back in place. He didn't have a clue what the outcome of the discussion would be, but after too many months of silence, Miguel was grateful he'd have the opportunity to finally talk about his feelings. "It's okay. Tonight's for Layla."

Layla came out with three glasses. "There was only one beer in the fridge, so we're splitting. And I dumped that half an ancient pizza in the garbage, Miguel. Jesus. How long has that been in there? It was growing shit."

He laughed. "I eat out a lot. Don't open the fridge much."

She handed each of them a glass, tapping hers to theirs. "Here's to us. And sex. And please, God," she said, her eyes raising heavenward as if in prayer, "many, many orgasms."

Miguel laughed at her toast, then took a drink. Finn did the same. Maybe it was misplaced hope, but Miguel was starting to think things might turn out okay.

Miguel drained his third of a beer in one chug, then took their glasses, placing them on the end table as well. He couldn't wait one more second. "Why don't we move this party to the bedroom?"

He wrapped his arm around Layla's waist, leading her down the hall. He glanced over his shoulder and noticed that, once again, Finn was right behind them, never missing a beat.

"The bed is made," Layla said, clearly surprised, given the state of his refrigerator.

"My mom always insisted that I make my bed every morning. I got in the habit and now I just do it without even thinking about it."

"That's sweet," she said.

Finn clearly didn't give a damn if the bed was made or not. He wasted no time reaching out and divesting Layla of her shirt. She turned toward Finn, his quick actions taking her by surprise.

"Damn, Finn. I like your style." She moved closer, intent on stripping off Finn's shirt as well, but he grasped her wrists, loosely pulling them behind her back in an alpha move that had Miguel's cock, which had already been hard, thickening even more.

Miguel was suddenly regretting letting his best friend off the hook—because he wanted Finn every bit as much as he wanted Layla, and he wasn't sure he'd manage to keep his hands on just her.

Finn shot him a quick warning look, reminding him of their agreement.

Dammit. His best friend knew him too well.

Miguel gave him a single nod, letting him know he was still on board with project Wild Side.

Finn turned his attention back to Layla.

"Not so fast, LJ," Finn murmured. "We've got all night. And we're going to take advantage of it."

Layla tried to still her racing heart, but it was impossible, especially when she tried to pull her hands free of Finn's hold. He tightened his grip...and holy fuck if the alpha move didn't have her pussy clenching almost painfully.

"I want to see you," she said, grimacing at the whiny tone in her voice.

Finn gave her a macho, self-confident grin that told her she wasn't going to get her way. And she wasn't going to be sorry about it.

"Let's get a few things straight before we start," Finn said.

Jesus. When did his voice get so deep and sexy? She shivered slightly, her arousal off the charts. "What things?"

"Miguel and I run the show. You want to broaden your horizons, expand on your sexual experiences. We know how to help you do that, but you have to trust us and do as we say."

Layla owned her own coffee shop because she didn't have the type of personality that allowed her to take orders. She preferred to be her own boss, to call the shots, to run the show.

But...that trait didn't seem to follow her into the bedroom. Or at least, not tonight. With Marco, she'd always taken the lead. Well, she had in the early days, when sex had been new and fun. The last couple of years, the bloom had been off that rose, and she hadn't initiated much of anything. Sex had become something they just did to scratch an itch, and even then, it felt more like a chore than pleasure.

"I do trust you." She glanced over her shoulder at Miguel. "I trust both of you."

Miguel gave her a quick wink before his gaze traveled back to Finn. It was obvious the cop had it bad for his best friend. She wasn't the only one totally turned on by this alpha Finn.

"Good." Finn released her hands. "Leave those by your side," he said, as he unfastened her bra, drawing it away from her breasts.

Second nature kicked in before Layla could think, her hands rising to cover herself.

This time, it was Miguel who captured her hands, drawing them down. "Don't hide yourself from us, Layla. You're beautiful." Miguel's grip was gentle, his thumbs caressing her palms in a sweet, reassuring, sexy way.

Finn cupped her breasts in his large hands, his grip possessive, rough. He plumped the flesh, then pinched her nipples.

Layla arched her neck, her head resting on Miguel's shoulder. He'd shifted closer, watching Finn's hands as they played with her breasts.

"Fuck, man," Miguel murmured when Finn pinched her nipples again, then lowered his head to suck one into his mouth.

Miguel ran his lips along the side of her neck, his tongue stroking the sensitive spot just behind her ear. He shifted the tiniest bit closer and she could feel his erection, still confined in his jeans, against her ass.

Layla pulled her hands free from Miguel's loose grip—and he let her—so that she could run her fingers through Finn's hair. She was torn between holding his lips to her breast forever and pushing him away, the sensations too good, too overwhelming. Orgasms were typically hard work, something she had to really concentrate on achieving. Now, surrounded by two of the sexiest, hottest guys she'd ever met, she felt perilously close to coming, simply from their mouths on her neck and breast.

"Need you," she whispered. "Please."

Finn lifted his head briefly, smiling. "I like the sound of that. Beg us some more, LJ."

It was obvious her begging was falling on deaf ears when he lowered his head once again, sucking her other nipple into his mouth, the suction so hard it sent a jolt of electricity from her tit to her pussy.

"God," she cried out, her fists closing in his hair, pulling it.

Finn groaned but didn't push away. Miguel was still kissing her neck, but his eyes were wide open, focused on everything Finn was doing to her.

"You've got gorgeous tits," Miguel murmured in her ear. "I can't wait for my turn to suck on those pretty nipples of yours."

She turned her head toward his, lips dancing along her cheek. One of his hands had found its way to her hair. He ran his fingers through it briefly before grasping a handful, pulling it the same way she'd just pulled Finn's.

Her cry of delight captured Finn's attention, and he lifted his head, watching as Miguel used his firm grip on her hair to hold her in place as he began kissing her neck again. Her eyes drifted closed in bliss, but not before she saw the hungry expression on Finn's face as he watched everything Miguel was doing to her.

They were slowly driving her out of her mind, relentlessly pushing her toward utter insanity, one tiny inch at a time.

Finn said he liked the sound of her begging, which was good. Because there was no way she could hold back her pleas. "I can't take it. Need you. Need you both. God. Now!"

She felt Finn's fingers unfasten the button of her jeans, then he unzipped them. "Toe off your shoes," he directed. She did so as he worked the denim and her panties over her hips. She kicked the material away when it dropped to her ankles.

It wasn't lost on her that she was totally naked, while both of them were fully dressed. She might have complained about that if Finn hadn't instantly dropped to his knees in front of her.

"Oh, holy fuck," she breathed as he lifted one of her legs and placed it over his shoulder, holding her open for his mouth. She jerked at the first contact, his tongue stroking her clit.

"Mother of God!"

Miguel chuckled at her exclamation. "We'll never have to guess where we stand with our girl, Finn."

She felt Finn's lips curve, a burst of hot breath hitting her pussy at his quiet laugh. He didn't say anything. Instead, he added his teeth to the game, nipping her clit. If Miguel hadn't been at her back, hadn't wrapped his strong arms around her in support, she might have fallen. She felt wobbly, light-headed as Finn deepened the suction on her clit.

"Please, please..." Her voice broke slightly on the second word. "Inside me. Gotta...have..."

Miguel moved his hands from her waist to her breasts, squeezing them with the same delicious roughness Finn had. Her nipples were hard enough to cut glass at this point.

Finn moved away from her, looking up to watch Miguel briefly before turning his attention back to her pussy.

He ran one finger along her slit, then lifted it toward Layla's mouth. Miguel released one of her breasts, quickly gripping Finn's wrist, the action taking both she and Finn by surprise. He drew Finn's finger to his mouth, sucking her arousal off.

Layla trembled, the image of Finn's finger in Miguel's mouth, the way Finn shuddered with need, making her dizzy.

"This is the best night of my life," she whispered.

Miguel released Finn's wrist, both men chuckling.

"We haven't even made it to the bed yet," Miguel pointed out.

She lifted one shoulder. "I don't care."

"Best night," Finn agreed.

She felt as if she could explode with joy, especially when Finn agreed. She'd been terrified she'd made a terrible mistake, agreeing to engage in a ménage right on the heels of Finn and Miguel's first kiss. But she'd seen the look in Miguel's eyes, the way he'd silently pleaded with her to say yes. She understood his reasons. Hell, she thought his idea was inspired.

Those fears she'd felt outside the pub vanished in the face of everything that had happened since then. Finn had never kissed another man, but there was no denying he had genuine, deep feelings for Miguel. Miguel, meanwhile, wore his heart on his sleeve. The second she'd seen him at the pub, his gaze locked on Finn's face, she'd recognized his desire.

The kiss had confused Finn. All he needed was a push in the right direction and a buffer for a brief time. Miguel wanted to be with Finn. A straight man. By bringing her into the bedroom with them the first time, he'd found a way to ease his friend into being with him.

Having her there provided Finn a way to slowly work up to what he wanted with Miguel, and it gave Miguel the chance to show Finn that he really did want this, even if he didn't realize it or want to admit it at the moment.

And, of course, there was the benefit to her. She'd love to play the selfless martyr card, but sweet Jesus. No one would believe that for a second. She wanted both men with a vengeance. Miguel's offer mirrored her fantasy and there'd been no way she could resist. She was going to steal this one night, steal all the pleasure, the bliss.

Finn's thumbs found her pussy, opening her. She'd never felt more exposed as he studied her. Her cheeks heated when he murmured the word "beautiful" before taking her clit back into his mouth.

This time, he added his fingers to the game, pushing two inside her. The lone leg supporting her weight buckled, but Miguel's strong arms held her up.

"I think we need to move this to the bed," he said to Finn.

Finn looked up and realized the impact his actions were having on her. His smug grin caused her to narrow her eyes, even though there was no denying he was wreaking havoc on her body.

"Good call," Finn said, lowering her leg and rising. Miguel surprised her when he bent and placed a muscular arm behind her knees, picking her up and carrying her to the bed. She'd never met such physically strong men. Both of them were considerably taller than her, though she wasn't a short woman. It was unusual for her to feel small in anyone's company, but right now, when she was flanked by these two mountains of muscle, she felt downright petite.

Miguel lay her down in the middle of the bed, then rose to stand beside the mattress. Finn was on the opposite side, and they both looked down at her.

She started to push herself up, but Finn placed a firm hand on her shoulder, holding her down.

"Stay there." The tone in his voice told her he expected her to do as he said, and she struggled to associate the easygoing friend she'd known for years with this commanding, take-no-prisoners man.

The contrary part of her longed to disobey, simply to see what Finn would do, but that idea flew out the window when he reached for the hem of his own T-shirt and pulled it off, revealing his bare six-pack abs.

"Fuck," she whispered.

She sort of expected both men to chuckle, but a quick glance in Miguel's direction told her he was just as turned on as she was. Then Miguel reached back and grasped the neck of his own shirt, pulling it off in one smooth move.

If Finn had a six-pack, Miguel had eight. He looked like he was chiseled from stone. The man would have been a Greek god back in mythological days. His skin was darker than Finn's, his Hispanic and black ethnicity revealed beautifully. He'd shared a bit about his family—his beloved mother, who hailed from Mexico. His father hadn't stuck around, and Miguel resented that, swore that he would never leave behind any kids he had.

Then he'd spoken highly of his powerhouse mother and the uncle who'd raised him to be the man he was today, and she'd been grateful he'd grown up in a house with so much love.

Like Miguel, Finn took a moment to study the other man's bare chest, and she realized they'd come to a moment of truth here. While the best friends had probably seen each other shirtless before, she doubted they'd witnessed each other completely naked and—given the large bulges beneath their jeans—fully erect.

"No guts, no glory," she said softly, hoping to ease the tension with humor.

It worked, as Finn rolled his eyes and started to unfasten his jeans. Miguel followed suit, both men looking at each other as they shed their pants. Finn was a boxer briefs guy, while Miguel went commando.

That was when she realized Finn and Miguel were big *everywhere*.

Once they were both naked, their attention turned back to her.

*What did I just sign on for?*

She suffered a split second of "what the fuck was I thinking?" before she came to her senses and realized she was seriously the smartest woman on earth for agreeing to this threesome. She lifted her arms in invitation.

Miguel placed one knee on the bed, then stopped. "I suppose we should do a condom count," he joked.

Finn reached down to grab the jeans he'd just shed and pulled out his wallet. He groaned. "I only have two."

Miguel opened his nightstand drawer. "I have three."

Layla giggled, thrilled that they both seemed to think that wasn't enough. "We'll be fine. I have six in my purse. So...I win."

Miguel and Finn broke into loud laughter.

Finn crawled on the bed, tugging her into his arms, kissing her senseless. She felt Miguel's weight on the opposite side, his hand stroking along her ribs, provoking a breathless laugh.

"That tickles," she said.

Miguel gripped her cheek, twisting her head until she faced him. "Stop hogging her," he said to Finn. Miguel's kiss was just as heated, just as sexy as Finn's.

Finn, undaunted to have her stolen away, reclaimed her breasts, sucking one of her nipples into his mouth again. He was clearly a boob guy, and she did not have a problem with that.

Layla tried to keep up, but both men were touching her, kissing her, exploring her. There were too many sensations at once. And the worst part was, they weren't touching the part that needed them most.

She snaked one hand lower, rubbing her clit a few times before pushing two fingers inside herself.

Finn lifted his head and growled an honest-to-God growl. The sound caught Miguel's attention and he broke the kiss, his gaze following where Finn was looking.

Finn gripped her wrist, halting her motion, though he didn't pull her fingers out. "Two of us in this bed with her, and she thinks she's going to get away with making herself come."

Miguel shook his head as if disappointed in what he was seeing. "This is a punishable offense."

She laughed, thinking they were joking, but the sound died quickly when neither man cracked a smile.

"You think this is funny?" Finn asked.

"I need to come," she said. "Like yesterday." Her tone was breezy and playful, and she hoped it would lighten what had suddenly become a fairly heated moment. They were looking at her too seriously.

"Sit up against the headboard," Finn said to Miguel. He moved without question. It was becoming pretty obvious who was going to call all the shots in the bedroom between Finn and Miguel. Layla tried to beat down the sudden sadness when she realized her time with them was limited, that the two of them would have a lifetime to explore each other's bodies, while she only had this night.

Finn gripped her hips, flipping her to her stomach with ease, reminding her once again of how strong he was. These men moved her into whatever position they wanted as if she weighed no more than a rag doll.

Firm fingers dug into her hips as Finn lifted her ass in the air. He'd positioned her between Miguel's outstretched legs, which left her face mere inches from the sexy cop's cock. She licked her lips. Miguel grinned and cupped her face affectionately.

"Wait for permission," he said.

"Give me permission," she demanded, her impatience getting the better of her. She'd always longed for more foreplay with Marco, feeling as if perhaps she'd been missing out on some of the best parts of sex. But she was coming to realize too much of a good thing really *was* too much. Her body ached, and if one of them didn't fuck her soon, she feared she'd go out of her damn mind.

Before Miguel could call her to task for her comment, Finn slapped her ass, the hard spank catching her by surprise.

"Ouch," she said, trying to shift away. Her ass stung.

Miguel held her in place as Finn lifted his hand and spanked her again. This time, he didn't pause in between; instead, placing half a dozen hard smacks on her ass and upper thighs. She struggled to get away through the first few, but when Finn pressed her knees apart and landed the next smack on her pussy, her back arched and she cried out for another.

Miguel lifted her face, kissing her cheeks and lips, lots of soft, quick kisses, while Finn continued to spank her. After a dozen or so smacks, he gave her exactly what she needed, driving two fingers inside her, hard and fast.

"Fuck!" Her back arched. God. She was right there. Right on the brink of—

Finn's fingers disappeared.

"No! Goddammit, Finn."

"Don't make me spank you again, LJ."

She laughed, even as his face darkened. "You don't seriously think that's going to scare me, do you?" she taunted.

"You hear this, man?" Finn asked Miguel, who shook his head, his smile wide and gorgeous.

Miguel shrugged. "You're running the show, bro. Do what you gotta do."

"What you gotta do," Layla said, looking over her shoulder at Finn, "is fuck me while I give Miguel a blowjob."

"Aaaaand," Miguel drawled, "I changed my mind. Layla's calling the shots."

The three of them laughed.

For a hot second.

And then, it just happened. Layla lowered her head and took Miguel into her mouth. Finn watched for a moment before she heard the crinkle of the condom wrapper. The head of his cock nudged against her opening, and she squeezed her eyes closed tightly, praying she could manage not to come on the first thrust.

She wanted this to last, but damn if she wasn't right there... this close.

Finn did not fuck around in the bedroom. The first inch penetrated, and then it was game on. He thrust in hard and fast and deep and holy fucking mother of God!

Layla tried to remember what she was doing, tried to concentrate on Miguel, on giving him a decent blowjob, but apparently, she was a selfish bitch. Or Finn was just that freaking good.

Miguel tugged her hair, drawing her mouth away from him. He kissed her, and his tongue mimicked the motion of Finn's cock inside her. Everything they did to her was in overdrive—fast and furious and perfect.

She came quickly, her body going stiff. Finn didn't even acknowledge the first climax.

Or the second.

He fucked her like a man possessed as she tried to keep up.

"Oh my God, Finn. Please! Jesus."

His fingers tightened on her hips and then, hallelujah, he was there with her.

"LJ. Brown Eyes. Baby." He came every bit as hard as she did. They froze for a split second. Then Finn fell next to her like a newly chopped tree.

Layla didn't—couldn't—move. She was supporting her weight on her elbows, her ass still up in the air. She looked up and saw Miguel's gorgeous eyes. He'd watched it all. Apart, but a part.

"Miguel," she whispered.

Finn, whose eyes had been closed, stirred as she said the other man's name, then he repeated it. "Miguel."

Miguel gently moved her, pressed her to her back on the soft mattress. He twisted with her. She wasn't sure when or where he'd gotten the condom, but he slipped it on. He came over her, caging her beneath him. "Say no if this isn't what you want, Layla."

His soft, kind voice made her smile. "I want you," she confessed.

Finn had propped himself up on one arm, facing them. "Make love to our girl," he urged Miguel. "I want to watch."

Layla had thought herself spent, too exhausted, done in. What a joke. Between Miguel's gentle touches and Finn's words, she was hotter now than she'd been all night.

Miguel slipped inside her, his motions softer, gentler. The impact was just the same.

*Fuck. Me.*

One night with these two men would never be enough. Yet, she couldn't ask for more. She knew what they were on the cusp of.

Hell, tonight was probably more than she should have taken. Not that she'd apologize for it.

Sorry, not sorry.

She lifted her arms to Miguel's shoulders, her nails scratching his skin. She raised her legs and locked her ankles around his waist. "Take me," she demanded. "I'm yours."

Miguel fucked her, slow and steady, his gaze never leaving hers. It felt as if he could see all the way to her soul, the connection between them so much deeper than anything she'd ever felt. They came together, the impact powerful. Potent.

Then she glanced over at Finn, wondering what he was thinking.

"That was—" Miguel started.

"Incredible," Finn whispered.

Layla smiled. "Best night ever."

$$\maltese \quad \text{IO} \quad \maltese$$

Layla opened her eyes, squinting against the sun shining through the window. It took her a second to orient herself. When she did, she realized she was alone in the bed.

Twice during the night, Miguel and Finn had woken up and taken her again. It had been drowsy, easy sex, but every bit as intense and incredible as the first time. Her body was sore, but damn if she wasn't still horny, still ready to go.

She sat up, wondering where the guys had gone, terrified they'd woken up with regrets. Miguel had invited her, but they were at the *beginning* of their relationship. Had she done the right thing by agreeing to come home with them?

She heard a shower shut off.

"Shit," she whispered to herself. She glanced around the room for her clothes, wondering if she could get dressed and escape before whoever had just finished showering came back. That idea was a brief one when Finn walked out of the bathroom with wet hair and a towel slung around his hips, at the same time Miguel entered from the hallway, a plate of buttered bagels in his hands.

"Feel like some breakfast in bed, you two?" Miguel asked, sitting on the edge of the bed.

Layla tucked the sheets around her tightly, trying to conceal her breasts, uncertain where she stood now in the cold, harsh light of day.

She reached for a bagel, realizing that Miguel was checking out Finn's bare chest. She might have felt offended if she wasn't drooling over said chest just as much.

"Well, that was fun," she said, trying to force a casual tone to her voice.

Miguel laughed. "Understatement of the century."

His words made Layla happier than they should. She hadn't lied about last night being the best of her life. She actually felt like a different person, completely changed, new.

"So...what's today's plan?" Finn asked.

Layla wasn't sure if his question was an invitation or a subtle hint that they should move on. The lighthearted tone made her think invitation, but she didn't want to assume that. "Have I overstayed my welcome?"

"What?" Miguel asked.

"Well...I mean," she stammered.

"LJ. I wasn't saying you should leave. I meant it. I want to know what our plan is for today. The three of us."

She liked the idea of spending more time with them, but the entire reason she was here was because Miguel and Finn had been skirting around the issue of their attraction to each other for God knew how long without talking about it. She wasn't going to make the same mistake. "Last night was only supposed to be a one-night stand. A jumping-in point for you guys. Not that you took advantage of it."

Now that she thought about it, Finn and Miguel hadn't made one bit of progress toward advancing their own physical relationship. So Miguel's plan had been a bust.

Instead of reaching for each other, they'd given her exactly what she'd hoped for. More—kinkier—sexual experiences.

She had hoped to make it easier for them to touch, to kiss, to be with each other. Instead, she'd been a distraction, an impediment to that goal.

"That might have been *your* purpose, LJ, but it wasn't ours, was it, Miguel?" Finn asked.

Miguel shook his head. "Not our purpose at all. I thought we were helping you explore your wild side."

She was struggling to figure out how she'd gotten so lucky. Not only were Finn and Miguel amazing lovers, they were seriously sweet guys...and they deserved to be happy.

While she'd definitely had the time of her life, she'd wanted to find a way to help these two kind, wonderful men find each other. "Well, on the wild side front, it was a slam dunk. I seriously thought my head was going to fly off my shoulders during one of those orgasms." She squeezed her legs together when her pussy started to flutter. "Just the thought of it..."

Finn sat down on the bed next to her and tugged down the sheet she was holding around her so he could palm her breast. "Lie down, Layla, and we'll do it all over again."

She was tempted. So damn tempted, but part of her got a sense Finn was deflecting, trying to avoid the conversation she'd just started. "The two of you didn't kiss again. You didn't..." She shrugged, letting them fill in the blanks.

"So, clearly we need more practice," Miguel said. "Another shot."

Finn chuckled. "I like where you're going with that, bro." He looked at Layla. "We need to give it another try, the three of us. Figure after thirty or forty attempts, we'll get there."

Layla laughed. "Don't tempt me. I'm not as good a person as I should be. I'll totally take you up on that."

"Wouldn't offer it if we weren't serious," Miguel said.

She studied both of their faces, trying to figure out if their offer was legit. "I'm not kidding, guys. Keep it up and I'll pencil you in for the next month or so."

Finn pinched her nipple, leaning forward to place a kiss on

her shoulder, one he followed up with a nip. "Not in pencil. Ink. Ink it in." He punctuated his comment by pulling her hair, drawing her head back so he could attack her neck.

She shook her head to dislodge his hand, shivering with arousal when his tongue stroked a line from her breast to just behind her ear. "I have to admit, I love this bad boy thing you've got going for you in the bedroom."

"So do I," Miguel admitted.

Finn grinned. "Good. Because tonight you're bringing home the cuffs, Miguel. We're going to play a little game of good cop/bad cop with our naughty LJ."

"Oh yeah. I can get behind that." Miguel leaned toward her and kissed her. "Promise you'll come back, Layla. We're not finished here. Not by a long shot."

She tried to figure out a way to refuse, but she wasn't a good enough person to say no to that offer. So...it looked like her wild side exploration was going into overtime.

Hell. Yeah.

Two hours later, Layla leaned on the counter of the coffee shop, trying to convince herself she'd made the right decision. She'd gone home with Miguel and Finn last night, thinking she'd expand on her sexual experiences, while helping two men who were clearly meant to be together find each other.

Somehow, the plan hadn't exactly worked out that way. She'd thought she could handle sex with no strings, thought she could separate emotions from the physical. That wasn't as easy as it sounded.

Which confused her. She'd grown up in a house full of horny, oversexed older brothers. And while they never talked to her about their sexual exploits, that didn't mean she hadn't eavesdropped on plenty of their "locker-room" talks over the years. They'd always made sex sound so hot...so easy. Love had rarely come into play. Instead, they'd described the physical pleasure, and she'd wanted to partake, to find the same.

She had last night. And then some.

Layla hadn't had a clue how bad the sex with Marco truly was until Miguel and Finn. Which was awesome. Until she found herself thinking about more than just the orgasms.

She recalled the sweet way Miguel cupped her cheeks when he kissed her. The way Finn had looked at her after they'd both come. The way they'd both called her "our girl."

Fuck.

This wasn't the way this was supposed to go down. Not even close. It was just sex. Just...fucking.

Yet Finn had told Miguel to "make love" to her, and damn if that wasn't exactly what it had felt like.

She shook her head, fighting to dislodge those words and these feelings.

The phone rang.

"Daily Grind. This is Layla. How may I help you?"

"You got robbed?"

She inwardly groaned when she heard Tony's voice. Of all her brothers, Tony—the oldest—was the most overprotective, and the one who'd been the most against her moving to Baltimore.

"Who told you?" she asked.

"I think the question is why didn't *you* tell us?"

She rolled her eyes, grateful Tony couldn't see her. He always lost his shit when she rolled her eyes at him. "It was nothing. I'm fine."

"I knew it was a bad idea for you to move to Baltimore. That place is a hotbed of crime."

"Oh for God's sake. This city was your home for the better part of your childhood. Stop being so melodramatic. A guy came in, pulled a gun, asked for money. He got a few hundred bucks and left. It's over and done with."

Layla didn't like the deathly silence that greeted her outburst. And when it was broken, she knew she'd fucked up.

"He had a gun?" Tony's tone was deathly quiet and slow.

Lord have mercy, she was screwed.

"Um. What did you hear?"

"I heard that the coffee shop had been robbed. I thought someone had broken in when the place was closed. You were *there?*"

Oh yeah. This wasn't going to end well. Tony would tell the rest of her brothers and her papa and by tonight, there would be a caravan of trucks parked outside her apartment, ready to move her back to Philly.

"I'm fine. As you can tell from the sound of my voice. Miguel showed up and—"

"Miguel?"

"He's the cop who responded after my 911 call. He's super nice, and he's been really good about keeping me in the loop on the case and coming by the shop a lot to—"

"You dating the cop?"

"No," she said quickly. Probably too quickly. Time to divert. "Besides, Finn is helping me put in a state-of-the-art security system, so the shop is going to be perfectly safe. I've handled it. Because I'm an *adult.*"

"Finn?"

Of course the only parts of her comments he heard were the male names. "Yeah. You remember Finn Young. We were friends in elementary school. His grandfather is Patrick Collins. They're a good family, and they've been looking after me since I've moved back."

Thank God. Maybe she'd found her way out of this mess. There was no way her brother would forget Patrick, and even if he did, her papa wouldn't. If they thought the Collins family had her back, she may have bought herself a reprieve.

It was times like this when she really missed her mama. She and Mama had been the only girls in a pack of hot-blooded, overprotective Italians. Despite that, her mama had ruled the roost, had known exactly how to handle her testosterone-laden men. So many times, Layla wished her mother had lived. She would have known how to control the Moretti men, would have convinced them that Layla wasn't some helpless female who couldn't survive on her own.

"Are you dating Finn?" Tony asked.

"No," she said. Talking to Tony was pretty much always like this. A frustrating third degree. She was anxious to get any thoughts of Miguel and Finn out of her brother's mind. It had taken Marco the better part of two years to win over her brothers, and it had been a long, painful process for the poor guy. There was no way she was subjecting Miguel or Finn to that, especially since they weren't dating.

They were just fucking.

Silently, she wished her answer was different. Wished Finn or —shit, *and*—Miguel were her boyfriends. But that wasn't what was happening. She was just the buffer...or the fluffer, ugh...or the middleman until Miguel and Finn were able to get their relationship off the ground.

"Joey and I are going to come see you this weekend. I want to check out this security system."

"No," Layla said, hotly. "Absolutely not! I'm working all weekend, and I don't have time to entertain you." That wasn't necessarily true. It wasn't work she didn't want her brothers to distract her from. "I'm telling you once and for all, I'm *fine*. I'm busy and happy and I don't need you hovering."

Tony didn't answer right away. And when he spoke again, she was surprised that he changed the subject. She'd really expected him to insist on the visit. "Saw Marco yesterday. He was asking about you. Worried about you."

"Tony. That's over. You know that's over."

"I know it is for you, but I'm not sure Marco is finding it as easy to let go. Are you sure—"

"I'm sure," she interjected. "I live in Baltimore now. Will you please believe me when I say I'm happy here?"

Tony sighed. "You still planning to come home for Thanksgiving?"

"I am," she said, knowing she had a snowball's chance in hell of keeping her brothers away from her until that holiday, though she was determined to try.

"Okay. If you need anything—" he started.

"I'll call," she reassured him. "I swear. I love you, lunkhead."

For the first time since he'd called, Tony chuckled. "I love you too, peanut."

She hated/loved her brothers' nickname for her, one derived from what they insisted was her peanut-shaped head when she was born.

They said their goodbyes and within two minutes, Layla was right back in the same funk she'd been in prior to Tony's phone call.

Her thoughts drifted to Marco. Tony said he'd asked about her. Marco had been totally ready to commit, to spend the rest of his life with her, and the very thought of that had turned her blood cold.

On the flip side, Miguel and Finn offered her exactly what she said she wanted. Sex with no strings, a chance to go wild. And while it was great, she couldn't help but wish for more.

So basically, she'd jumped from the frying pan right into the fire.

Because...of course she did.

❧ 11 ❧

Finn let himself into Miguel's apartment. He had his own key to the place and had for the better part of a year. Miguel had called him a half hour earlier to say he was running late, trying to finish up some paperwork at the precinct. Layla wouldn't close the coffee shop for another twenty minutes, so he had the place to himself for a little while.

He wasn't happy about that. He'd already had too many hours alone today, stuck in his own head. Fergus had called in sick this morning. Not that Finn believed for a second his cousin was under the weather. Aubrey was taking off again tomorrow for another gig, which meant she'd be out of town for a few days. Fergus, the sex-craved lunatic, had clearly managed to keep his fiancée and love of his life in bed all day.

While Finn was happy—fuck, he was trying really hard to be happy—for his cousin, the day alone in the office had left him too much time to dissect and analyze every goddamn thing that had happened last night. From Miguel showing up at the pub, to the kiss he'd shared with his best friend, to the blow-his-fucking-mind sex he'd had with Layla, he'd struggled to make it through the day. His emotions were all over the place. He was horny, freaked out, confused, horny, excited, thrilled, horny and fucked the fuck up.

He had promised Miguel they'd talk about that kiss they'd shared, but God only knew what he'd say. Finn had never kissed another man, had never even considered such a thing. And he sure as shit hadn't expected to be so...*moved* by it. That kiss had rocked the very foundation of his world.

Then Layla had stepped forward and added her kiss to the mix, and damn if hers hadn't shaken him right to the core as well.

Miguel had suggested the threesome, Layla had said yes, and Finn—weak fucking bastard that he was—had followed them like a puppy dog because his dick had been doing all the thinking.

Given the fact he was currently sitting in Miguel's living room with a hard-on that could drive stakes into the ground, it was safe to say his cock was still serving as his brain.

Last night, with Miguel and Layla, he'd experienced something he'd never anticipated or expected. It had been the most incredible night of his life, and even as he admitted that to himself, he knew they'd only scratched the surface.

The door to the apartment opened and Miguel stepped in. He looked distracted and a little stressed out until he spotted Finn, sitting in the living room.

"Oh, hey, man."

"Rough day?" Finn asked.

Miguel shrugged. "No. Yes. I can't solve this fucking robbery case and it's pissing me off. The guy pulled a gun on Layla. I want to find the dude and kick his ass, lock him up. Instead, I'm buried in paperwork, following one damn dead end after another. The promotion list comes out next month, and if I can't crack this fucker..."

"You're going to solve it," Finn said, hating how despondent his best friend sounded. "You're an amazing cop and you're going to catch the guy. I don't doubt it for a second."

Miguel's face cleared, and he gave Finn a ghost of a smile. "Thanks, man. Hey, give me a minute to get out of my uniform."

Finn nodded as Miguel drifted down the hall. He sank down on the couch and waited. Miguel reappeared a few minutes later in jeans and an old Korn T-shirt he'd clearly stolen from Finn.

"I've been looking for that shirt."

Miguel chuckled, but offered no apology. "Guess you found it."

Silence fell between them, and Finn knew they'd reached the moment of truth. The kiss they'd shared the night before lingered between them, the giant elephant in the room.

"Listen—" Finn started.

Before he could say more, there was a knock at the door.

Miguel left the living room and went to answer it. Finn heard Layla's voice before he saw her. "Hey. I know I'm early, but I couldn't spend one more second in that coffee shop. You promised me handcuffs."

Miguel was laughing as he and Layla entered the living room, and her face lit up when she saw Finn. Her smile when she spotted him did something funny to his heart. Actually, just standing in this room with Miguel and Layla took away all the heavy feelings he'd been trapped under all day. Suddenly, he felt lighter, happier, ready to take on the world.

Miguel reached into the back pocket of his jeans and pulled out his cuffs, twirling them playfully on one finger.

Layla tossed her purse on the coffee table and took off her jacket. "You're not wasting any time," she teased, pointing to the handcuffs.

Finn had spent the better part of two hours thinking about this moment, this fantasy, and he had some definite ideas about how he wanted it to play out. He adopted a stern expression and crossed his arms.

Layla gave him a curious look. She didn't realize the game had begun.

Finn walked over and took the cuffs from Miguel, then he

grasped Layla's upper arm and led her out of the living room. She grinned, quickly following, expecting him to move them all to the bedroom. He tightened his grip on her arm to stop her from going all the way down the hall to Miguel's room.

He shook his head, then jerked it toward the kitchen. "In here, Ms. Moretti. Officer Garcia and I are going to do our interrogation in this room."

Layla giggled, but Finn was careful to school his expressions, to give the appearance of a serious cop. It wasn't that hard to do. After all, he'd been raised by a cop, and he'd been on the receiving end of some pretty intense questioning whenever he'd done something bad in high school. Dad was a master interrogator.

Miguel followed them, leaning against the doorframe, his arms crossed, watching as Finn set the stage for this fantasy.

Finn pulled a chair into the middle of the room and Layla started to sit down. He stopped her. "No. Take off your clothes."

Layla glanced around, suddenly looking slightly nervous. Miguel's apartment was on the fourth floor, and while the blinds on the window were open, there was no building across the street. No way anyone could look in and see her.

"I suggest you cooperate, Ms. Moretti. It'll go easier for you if you do." Finn stepped behind Layla, who hadn't started to take off her clothes. He threw a covert wink at Miguel, who was definitely giving off some intimidating cop vibes. The corners of Miguel's mouth twitched, but he was careful not to let Layla see.

"We're waiting, Ms. Moretti," Finn prodded.

Layla glanced over her shoulder at him, and he recognized the twinkle in her eye. She was ready to play. She slowly pulled her shirt up and over her head. She tossed it at him and Finn quickly caught it. Her bra followed, but she tossed that sexy scrap of lace at Miguel.

Her shoes and jeans went next, and finally her panties.

"How's that for cooperation?" she said, her voice breathless and sexy as fuck.

Finn's cock thickened at the sight of her beautiful naked body. He'd spent way too much time playing out this fantasy today. He needed to get control of himself or this would be over before it started.

He placed a strong hand on her shoulder and pressed her down into the chair. Then he reached for her wrists, drawing them behind her back. He slapped the cuffs on. With her hands bound behind her, her breasts were pushed out, and he was helpless to resist copping a feel, pun intended. He cupped one of her tits and squeezed it, loving the way her eyes drifted closed, the soft exhalation of pleasure.

"Open your eyes and look at me," he demanded roughly.

Her eyes flew open, but there was no fear there. In fact, the saucy little minx actually winked at him, grinning mischievously.

Finn sighed heavily, shaking his head as he glanced over his shoulder at Miguel. "Ms. Moretti doesn't appear to understand the seriousness of this situation."

Miguel pushed away from the door and crossed the room to her. "Then I guess it's up to us to show her."

Miguel bent and pressed Layla's knees apart. "Wrap your ankles around the legs of the chair."

She did as he asked, but Miguel still wasn't satisfied. He gripped her ass and tugged her forward on the seat.

"Stay there," Miguel said. "Don't move." Miguel rose and stood behind her, his hands on her shoulders. It was a power move, another way to make Layla feel captured, trapped. Miguel gave Finn a look that said, "your turn."

Finn knelt in front of her, his gaze drifting to her pussy. "You've been a very bad girl," he said, adopting a deep voice.

Layla shook her head. "It wasn't me," she said, getting into the spirit of the role play. "I was set up. You've got the wrong person."

"No. I don't think we do. We have ways to make you confess." Finn reached out and drew his finger along her slit, teasing her clit for just a second or two.

Layla's hips lifted toward his touch.

He placed a quick slap on her inner thigh. "Officer Garcia told you not to move."

"God, Finn," she breathed.

He slapped her other thigh. "That's Officer Young to you," he corrected. "Understood?"

"Yes, sir."

"Now, we're going to need to search you."

She smiled. "I'm naked. What could I possibly be hiding, Officer?"

Finn didn't respond. Instead, he thrust two fingers inside her, eliciting a gasp from her pretty pink lips.

He crooked his fingers and found her G-spot. Layla's hips lifted again. Finn feigned disappointment at her movement as he withdrew his fingers.

Layla narrowed her eyes. "No. Don't stop."

Miguel's hands tightened on her shoulders as he bent lower, his lips right by her ear. "You don't make the rules here, Ms. Moretti. We do."

Fuck. Finn had intended to come in here and seduce the hell out of Layla, but he was the one being seduced by them. He was so fucking turned on, he wasn't sure he'd be able to play this out until the end.

Miguel must have noticed his distress. "I think it's time we teach Ms. Moretti how to control her mouth."

Finn stood up and unbuttoned his jeans. "I think you're right." He pushed his pants and boxer briefs to his knees, then shifted closer to Layla.

She licked her lips and moved toward him as much as she could.

"Open your mouth, Ms. Moretti," Miguel said, his face next to Layla's. Both of them were close to Finn, to his cock.

He stepped between her outstretched legs and pressed the head of his dick into her mouth. Miguel didn't move away.

Instead, he placed a soft kiss on Layla's cheek. "Run your tongue along the bottom of his cock."

Layla did as Miguel instructed, and Finn saw stars.

"Suck him," Miguel murmured in her ear. "Suck him hard. He's a tough cop. He can take it."

Layla was very good—too fucking good—at following instructions. Finn grabbed one handful of her hair, using that grip to push deeper into her mouth.

"Open your throat. Take him deeper. Swallow the head."

"Fuck," Finn muttered. "Miguel." He hoped his friend would take the hint and back off on the directions a little. He needed him to understand how close he was to blowing.

Layla did exactly what Miguel told her to, his cock brushing the back of her throat, and he knew he was a goner. He started thrusting faster, deeper, Layla right there with him, her tongue and lips driving him insane.

Finn didn't want to come. Not this soon. He started to pull out— but froze when Miguel reached out and gripped the base of his cock.

None of them moved as time literally stood still. Finn looked down at his best friend's fist wrapped around his cock, the head of his dick in Layla's mouth. His heart thudded so loudly, it deafened him.

The three of them simply remained there, locked together.

And then...something broke loose.

In all of them.

Finn thrust, pumping his dick in Miguel's hand and Layla's mouth. Layla sucked him harder as Miguel tightened his grip.

"Fuck!" Finn shouted, his balls constricting. There was no holding back, no stopping. He pulled Layla's hair harder and she groaned, the sound reverberating against his flesh. He pulled out and exploded, coming with the force of a freight train, painting Layla's breasts with his come.

Miguel let go, reaching behind Layla and unlocking the cuffs. The metal clanged against the kitchen floor as they fell. Miguel rubbed her shoulders, kissed the top of her head, whispered sweet words to her.

Finn watched Layla, unable to force himself to look at Miguel. He was struggling to find his footing. None of this fantasy had played out the way he'd intended. He wasn't creative enough, inventive enough, to have ever imagined something that hot.

Finn pulled up his jeans but didn't bother to zip them as he shifted toward the sink. His feet felt like they were made of wood, his body still trying to recover from the intensity of his climax.

He reached for a paper towel, wetting it, then returning to Layla to wipe his come off her breasts.

She smiled at him, the look, one of pure joy. "That was amazing," she said softly. "I like role play...a lot."

He nodded, even though her description was nowhere near enough to touch what had just happened.

Finn kissed her, and then he looked at Miguel. His best friend stared back at him, his shoulders stiff, his fists clenching and unclenching.

Miguel looked as if he was expecting Finn to throw a punch.

Jesus. He really *had* fucked things up. His silence these past few months had been nothing short of cruelty. He'd hurt Miguel deeply.

Finn couldn't do that anymore.

He reached out and gripped the back of Miguel's neck. His friend stiffened, but Finn pressed on, dragging Miguel toward him.

And kissed him.

## ❧ 12 ❧

It took Miguel a full thirty seconds to figure out that Finn was kissing him. Like *really* kissing him.

After too many months of avoidance, of wanting something he never thought he'd get, it was taking him a hell of a long time to wrap his head around this kiss.

When he figured it out, he gripped Finn's hips, pulling him closer, deepening the kiss. Finn didn't shy away. Instead, he opened his mouth, stroking Miguel's lower lip with his tongue. His fingers dug into the back of Miguel's neck, holding him almost possessively. Then they loosened, and Finn slowly stepped away.

Miguel studied his face, waiting for the other shoe to drop, for Finn to change his mind.

It didn't happen. Finn gave him a small smile. "Sorry for…"

"For?" Miguel prompted, praying Finn wasn't about to apologize for kissing him.

"For the past few months."

Miguel breathed a sigh of relief, an airy laugh.

"Well. I guess my work here is done." Layla stood, and it became clear she intended to get dressed and leave.

Miguel and Finn moved at the same time, caging her between them.

"Where do you think you're going?" Finn asked.

Layla tilted her head, adorably confused when she said, "Home?"

"The fact that you made that answer a question proves you know you're not going anywhere except to my bed," Miguel responded. Then he decided to change the pronoun. "*Our* bed."

Layla shook her head slowly, ready to protest, but Miguel didn't give her the chance. He kissed her—a hard, fast touch of his lips—before he cupped her face and held her gaze. "This isn't over yet, Layla."

She blinked a couple of times. "But—"

"But nothing. Miguel's right. This isn't over." Finn grasped her hand, then pointed to the handcuffs on the floor. "You better bring those," he said to Miguel. "Just in case our girl tries to escape."

Miguel chuckled as he picked up the cuffs, following Finn and Layla to the bedroom, grateful they'd convinced her to stay.

Shit. He was going to have to figure out what the hell that meant eventually. But not tonight.

Tonight was too perfect, and he wasn't going to ruin it by thinking.

He grinned at the absurdity of that rationalization.

Finn led Layla straight to the bed, pulling back the covers for her. She crawled into the middle of the mattress and Miguel soaked up the sight. She still looked slightly uncertain, and Miguel didn't like it.

He pulled off his shirt and climbed onto the bed next to her. Time to distract her from thinking as well.

He cupped her cheek and kissed her, his tongue stroking her lips, her teeth. She tasted sweet, and he suspected she'd treated herself to one of the desserts she sold at the coffee shop.

The mattress dipped as Finn joined them on the bed. His friend had stripped off his clothes as he and Layla kissed.

Miguel stood as Finn took over the kisses, watching the two of them while he removed his jeans, but he didn't return to the bed once he was naked, too spellbound by them.

He leaned against the post of the footboard, enjoying the show.

Finn was a surprise in the bedroom, confidant and commanding. Miguel hadn't really expected that. In their everyday lives, Miguel was the stronger of the two, the one who tended to take control of what they did, where they went. Finn was the type to just go with the flow.

That didn't translate to the bedroom. Not even a little.

Finn's lips traveled along Layla's neck, not stopping until he'd reached her breasts. He pinched one hard nipple as he sucked on the other. Layla's back arched as he alternated between tiny bites of pain followed by soothing pleasure.

"Please," Layla whispered. Miguel grinned at the desperation in her tone. Patience wasn't her strong suit, as she tried to race through the foreplay.

Finn chuckled darkly. "You want our cocks inside you, Brown Eyes?" he murmured. Miguel liked Finn's term of endearment for her. A lot.

She nodded. "So much."

"Too soon," Finn said.

Layla closed her eyes, the sound that slipped out pure whine. "I can't wait. I don't want to wait."

"She's spoiled," Miguel said with a grin.

Finn glanced over at Miguel. He knew neither Finn nor Layla had forgotten he was there. In fact, he'd noticed the way Finn had angled them on the bed, giving Miguel a bird's-eye view of the action.

"Think we should put her out of her misery?" Finn asked him.

Miguel shook his head. "I don't think she's suffered enough."

Layla flashed a dirty look his direction, while Finn laughed.

"I agree." Finn shifted lower on the bed, drawing Layla's legs over his shoulders as he bent down and sucked her clit into his mouth.

"Fuck. Me," Layla whispered, though Miguel couldn't tell if it was a demand or a curse.

Finn pushed two fingers inside her pussy, stroking her half a dozen times, pushing her to the edge before withdrawing.

Layla pounded her fists on his shoulders. "Dammit, Finn!" Then her attention turned to Miguel, her sultry gaze traveling south, smiling when she saw his erection. Miguel ran his fists along the sensitive flesh, gathering pre-come with the tips of his fingers.

Finn finger-fucked her slowly, keeping her body on a steady hum, while ensuring she couldn't fly over the peak.

Layla licked her lips. "Miguel. I want you inside me. Fucking me hard and fast."

She thought he'd be easier to sway. She was wrong, but he let her believe she'd won when he climbed back onto the bed. He took one of her legs off Finn's shoulders, opening her even wider. He pressed one finger inside her wet heat next to Finn's, stretching her.

Then he pulled it out, moving his wet finger lower, circling her anus.

Her hips reared up even as she sought to move away.

Finn gripped her thigh, holding her in place for Miguel's exploration.

"Mmmm," he hummed, pressing until he was one-knuckle deep in her ass. He wiggled it, thrilled when she moaned—the sound sheer pleasure—then she pushed toward his finger, trying to take in more.

"Fuck," Finn muttered. "You look so hot with Miguel's finger in your ass, LJ. Do you like it?"

She nodded, the motions jerky, her face flushed a bright red, her breathing erratic. "I...need..."

"We know what you need, Brown Eyes." Finn's fingers moved inside her, but it was still too slow. "And we're going to give it to you. All of it. But we can't do this in one night. We need more time."

Miguel grinned. Finn had led her to this place intentionally, driving her completely out of her mind, distracting her by withholding her orgasm, and now he was going in for the kill.

Layla blinked, trying to focus, trying to regain her wits.

Miguel couldn't let her do that. He pushed his finger deeper into her ass, not stopping until it was lodged to the hilt.

"Oh my God," she breathed. "Please!"

"Don't you see, LJ," Finn persisted. "There's still so much we can teach you. Say you'll give us more time."

"How much?" she asked, the question ending with a squeak when Miguel curled his finger in her ass.

Finn looked at him, letting Miguel set the time frame.

It was on the tip of Miguel's tongue to suggest a year or three, but he knew Layla would balk at that. Hell, she'd probably consider even a month too long.

"A week," Miguel said. It wasn't enough...but maybe at the end of it, they could convince her to give them another.

"A week," Finn repeated. "We'll squeeze every sexual adventure we can into seven days. We're going to drive each other wild."

Layla's cheeks were pink, her chest rising and falling. "I don't—"

Miguel pulled his finger out of her ass, then thrust in again, rapidly, rougher. At the same time, Finn curled his fingers in her pussy.

"Fuck," she gasped. "You guys don't play fair."

"Never said we would," Miguel responded, prompting Finn to laugh. He loved the sound.

"Fine. One week, but if you want me to leave—" Her words died again when Finn pulled his fingers out of her completely and Miguel followed suit.

"Hey," she protested.

Finn lowered his head and licked her slit, one long, slow

stroke. Miguel wondered what it would feel like to be on the receiving end of that wickedly talented tongue. Though Finn had initiated the kiss in the kitchen earlier, Miguel still felt an invisible barrier between them in bed.

It was one thing to kiss a guy. It was another thing to fuck him.

Obviously, Finn was still struggling with taking that next step. And Miguel understood. Having Layla here with them was definitely going to make that easier.

Finn pressed his tongue inside Layla's pussy, and Miguel decided now was a good time to push some boundaries.

He ran his hand over Finn's bare ass.

Finn froze, just for a second, his gaze sliding toward Miguel. Then he returned his attention to Layla.

Okay. So far, so good.

Miguel repeated the action, stroking Finn's ass several times before going for broke. He ran his finger along the slit between Finn's ass cheeks, introducing him to the same anal play he'd just initiated with Layla.

Finn didn't try to get away. Instead, he kept tongue-fucking Layla. Their positions on the bed left Miguel at a disadvantage because he couldn't see Finn's face, couldn't tell if he liked the touch or was merely tolerating it for him.

He'd spent too many months wanting this, wanting Finn. His patience was in tatters. He needed to know.

Miguel pressed the tip of his finger in Finn's ass.

Once again, Finn stilled, for just a moment. Then he lifted his head and looked at Miguel. "Shove it in there like you mean it, Miguel. Just do me a favor. Find some lube."

Fuck. Miguel was going to come. Just from the goddamn invitation.

Layla giggled and tried to sit up.

Finn held her to the bed. "Where do you think you're going?"

"I can't see anything from down here."

Finn growled. "Tough. I'm still hungry."

"We'll give you a show later," Miguel promised as he reached into his nightstand drawer for a tube of lubrication.

"Just your finger," Finn said.

Miguel realized his friend was nervous, but he wasn't shying away from this, from what they could and—please God—would do to each other.

"You got it," Miguel said. "But just so you know, I like something a little bigger in *my* ass." Miguel had taken both roles in bed with his male lovers—the giver and the receiver. He enjoyed both, but if he had to claim a favorite position, it was definitely the receiver. And given Finn's dominance in the bedroom, Miguel didn't doubt he was going to love every second of Finn's cock buried deep in his ass as he whispered those sexy demands of his.

Finn didn't respond to Miguel's confession, but Layla did. "Oh my God. You guys are so fucking hot."

Miguel bent down and gave her a quick kiss on the cheek, as he tried to imagine this same scenario without Layla there. Something told him neither he nor Finn would be quite as at ease. He wasn't entirely sure what that meant, but in some weird, twisted way, it made sense. After all, until him, Finn had been completely straight. And given his abilities in the bedroom, there was no denying, Finn liked having sex with a woman—a lot. The same held true for Miguel. He'd had his fair share of male and female lovers, and he couldn't say he preferred one sex over the other.

While he loved primal, rough sex with a man, there was a lot to be said for being with a sweet, soft, sexy woman as well.

With Layla in their bed, he got the best of both worlds.

Shit.

That realization crashed down on him like a two-ton weight. Miguel wanted Layla in the bed—not as a buffer, but because she fit here. With them.

"You okay, bro?" Finn asked, drawing him out of his head.

He nodded, unwilling to ruin tonight by worrying. He and

Finn had convinced Layla to stay another week. They had time. Time for Miguel to discover if Finn wanted to keep her as well. And then, if so, time for the two of them to convince her they were more than wild enough to keep her happy.

Finn bent his head to Layla once more, sucking her clit into his mouth as he pushed two fingers inside her. Layla's back arched and her eyes drifted closed.

That was as much as Miguel watched. Then he opened the lube, coated his finger, and pressed it to the hilt in Finn's ass in one smooth, nonstop motion.

"Shit," Finn breathed against Layla's pussy, shifting his ass higher in obvious invitation.

Miguel thrust in and out, loving it when Finn picked up the rhythm, pushing back to take more of him inside.

"Add another one," Finn demanded after several minutes, his words hoarse, breathy.

Miguel watched as Finn gave Layla exactly what *he'd* just asked for, pressing a third finger inside her, stretching, filling her.

Miguel covered his middle finger with lube, then slid it in next to the first. He didn't bother with gentleness. Finn clearly wasn't looking for that.

"We're getting finger-fucked," Finn said to Layla. "And we're going to come this way. Together. Then you and I are going to take turns sucking Miguel's cock."

Jesus! Miguel bit the inside of his mouth hard enough to draw blood, needing the pain to keep from coming just at the thought of getting a blowjob from both his lovers.

He picked up the speed, plunging his fingers in Finn's ass harder. Finn repeated the same motion on Layla, her head tossing back and forth on the pillow as she plummeted toward her climax.

She came loudly, Finn right on her heels as he gripped his cock, stroking it firmly, three, four times before come spurted out, covering her stomach.

Miguel started to pull out, then reconsidered, curving his

fingers, finding Finn's prostate. His best friend jerked with renewed arousal as Miguel withdrew.

"Motherfucker," Finn cursed. "Miguel!"

There was nothing sweeter than the sound of his name on Finn's lips. Or so Miguel thought, until Layla's soft hand wrapped around the base of his cock. Miguel grabbed a tissue and wiped the lube from his fingers, then he ran his hand through her long, dark hair, gripping it the way Finn had their first night together. She liked having her hair pulled, liked it when they used that grip to pull her to them.

Layla opened her mouth and took Miguel inside, pressing her tongue firmly to that spot, just under the head of his dick, that drove him crazy. She'd recalled his instructions from earlier, and now she was using his own lessons on how to give a blowjob against him.

Finn knelt next to her, but didn't try to move in. Instead, he reached around and gripped Miguel's ass, his fingers working their way through his ass cheeks until he found Miguel's anus. He didn't try to breach him, settling instead for simply stroking the sensitive hole, the touch more promise than provocation.

"This isn't going to take long," Miguel admitted, perfectly aware there was nothing he could do to bank the fire raging inside him. Watching Layla and Finn come, fingering Finn's ass, the incredible way Layla was sucking his cock. He'd been too close for too long.

"Don't hold back, man," Finn said. "We've got all night." Then he grinned. "We've got a week."

Miguel exploded, Layla holding him in her mouth, swallowing down his come.

Fuck.

A week.

That would never be enough.

## ❧ 13 ❧

Layla lay on the couch, her head on Finn's lap as he mindlessly toyed with her hair, his attention riveted to the hockey game on TV. He had a twenty-dollar wager with his cousin Colm on the outcome, and the Collins family took their bets very seriously.

Miguel sat on the opposite end of the couch, her bare feet in his lap, and he gently rubbed them. Like Finn, he was completely absorbed in the game, so Layla had some time to study their faces. Memorize them just as they were. Just like this.

Tonight marked the end of their week. Night number seven.

Layla had played a game with herself all week, told herself what they were doing was just casual, fun, easy. She figured if she said it enough, she'd believe it.

So much for that.

On Wednesday, Finn and Miguel had decided to resume what was apparently their weekly self-defense, tactical attack night. Only this week, they'd included her in the lessons. After the robbery attempt in the coffee shop, both men thought she needed to know some self-defense moves. They'd taken their teaching very seriously, and Miguel was delighted by how quickly she picked it all up. Finn was less amused, especially when she managed to escape his grip when he pretended to attack her from behind. She allowed herself to go slack in his hold, pulling him off-balance, then she kicked back and actually managed to knock him to his knees.

Miguel had laughed so hard tears streamed down his face, as Finn grumbled something about now having to deal with two of them kicking his ass every week. It had been a lot of fun.

Everything with them was fun.

She turned her gaze toward the game, wishing she could become as engrossed in it as the guys. It might be nice to actually find a way to turn off her brain for an hour or so. The only time this week she'd managed to accomplish that was when Miguel and Finn had her naked in bed, finding creative, earth-shaking, bone-rattling new ways to fuck her. She'd lost count of how many orgasms she'd had over the course of the week, but it had to be in the upper double digits range.

It had been the best week of her life, hands down. And now it was over.

She'd already insinuated herself into Finn and Miguel's budding relationship for far longer than she should have. When Miguel had suggested they all go to bed together, she'd truly believed it would just be the one night. One night to help the guys find their way to each other, and then she'd bail out.

She'd been determined to keep sex simple. One-night stands, casual sex. A way to broaden her sexual horizons without losing her heart...or another five years of her life.

Miguel and Finn had given her that.

Had offered sex without strings

Had introduced her to kinks and positions she didn't even know existed.

Had ruined her for all other men.

Ugh.

Finn had meant those words as a joke, but damn if she wasn't afraid they were true.

No. She refused to believe that.

She only thought it was true because Miguel and Finn were much better lovers than Marco. That didn't mean they were the best in the world, though God help her if she found anyone better. She'd spontaneously combust.

Layla silently cursed herself for being an idiot, for succumbing to this stupid depression. There were more fish in the sea, and starting tomorrow, she'd put herself back out there and continue to do what she'd started with Miguel and Finn.

Her unencumbered year was in full swing.

Plus, she still had tonight with Finn and Miguel, and she planned to take advantage of that.

Grinning, she decided to see if she could distract her guys from their hockey game.

She shifted her foot slightly, running it over the crotch of Miguel's lounge pants, teasing his cock with her toes. It took less than a minute for him to go stiff, for his gaze to shift to her, his grin knowing, his eyes hungry.

She gave him a playful wink, then pretending to stretch, her hand landing on the front of Finn's pants. She stroked him, making the touch appear absentminded rather than calculated, even as she pressed her foot harder against Miguel.

The sexy cop held her foot to him and started lifting his hips, applying more pressure to her actions.

He wasn't watching the game anymore, his eyes locked on her face.

She gazed upwards, wondering if Finn was even aware of the game of footsie she and Miguel were playing. She was surprised to discover he'd given up on the hockey game as well. He was watching the action in Miguel's lap. When he felt her eyes on him, he reached down and lifted the hem of her T-shirt, pulling it over her breasts.

She'd stripped off her bra about five minutes after arriving here. Neither she nor Finn had been back to their own apartments this week, the three of them sharing Miguel's bed night after night.

Finn's fingers latched onto one of her nipples and he pinched it tightly. The pressure was a trigger, sending electricity straight to her pussy. And Finn, the clever man, knew it.

"I think our girl is getting bored," Finn said.

Layla loved it when they called her "our girl" and "Brown Eyes." She also loved the way they looked at her like she was the most beautiful woman on earth, the way they each managed to stop by the coffee shop for a few minutes each day, just to smuggle her back to her office to steal kisses. She'd spent years with Marco and never gotten a sense that he thought that much about her when she wasn't around. Meanwhile, Finn and Miguel always acted as if they'd been away from her years rather than hours, and the smiles that lit up their faces when they first saw her at the end of the day never failed to touch her.

"You can watch the hockey game," she said, deepening the pressure on both their cocks—with her hand and her foot. "I can find ways to entertain myself just fine."

Finn gripped her wrist, pressing her hand against his dick harder as he pinched her nipple again. "Thought we talked about that before, told you we didn't want you entertaining yourself. Not with us here."

"Well, it's the end of our week. Chances are pretty good there will be the occasional night or two where I'll have to take care of business myself after this."

Finn narrowed his eyes and for a moment, she thought perhaps she'd upset him. Ignoring it, she decided he was ramping up their play. Finn was a master at role play. Ever since he and Miguel had treated her to their kinky version of good cop, bad cop, they'd also assumed the roles of professors to her naughty schoolgirl and demanding CEOs to her sexy secretary. They'd taken her on the kitchen table, the living room floor, over the desk in Miguel's home office, and three times in the shower.

"I didn't realize you'd been counting down the days," Miguel said.

Damn. She sat up slowly, pulling her feet away from his lap.

"I haven't," she lied. "I'm just saying…I'm very good at entertaining myself." She hoped her sultry tone and playful grin would help put them back on track. She didn't want to think about ending things with them tomorrow. She was determined for one more mind-blowing night of sex.

"Is that right?" Finn asked. "Show us."

Layla tilted her head. "You want me to masturbate in front of you."

"Where's the vibrator you brought over the other night?" he asked.

The three of them had gotten into a discussion about sex toys a few nights earlier, and Layla had confessed to having a favorite vibrator. Finn had convinced her to pack it in her overnight bag and they'd used it on her for hours, giving her three orgasms with just the toy before finally taking her.

"It's in the bedroom." She hadn't taken it home, in hopes that maybe they could do a repeat performance of that night.

"Go get it," Finn said, using that demanding tone that never failed to make her wet.

"I—"

"He's not going to repeat the request, Brown Eyes," Miguel said in such a way that she knew her comment about the week ending had been forgotten. While Finn was clearly the more dominant of the two men, Miguel had assumed the role of second-in-command. Miguel would follow Finn's orders in bed, but he always managed to issue his own demands when it came to what he wanted from Layla. Funny how in this one instance, she had no problem being low man on the totem pole.

She stood up and went to the bedroom, grabbing the vibrator. They wanted to watch her use it on herself, and she flushed at the thought. Not with embarrassment, but with excitement.

Layla started to leave the bedroom, then stopped. If she was going to give them a show, she wanted it to be memorable. Stripping out of her shirt and lounge pants, she tugged her ponytail free, pulling her hair loose over her shoulders.

"What's taking so long?" Finn called out from the living room.

She rolled her eyes at his impatience, but didn't call him on it. She crossed the room to the nightstand and pulled out the bottle of lubrication. She wasn't the only one performing tonight.

While Finn and Miguel had added countless sexual experiences to her repertoire, they'd been slower to expand on their own...with each other.

Anal play had become part of their nightly routine, but so far, neither man had breached the other with more than fingers. And so far, she'd given the only blowjobs, her fellas going no further than hand jobs. She knew they wanted to do more, but something was holding them back.

Miguel had invited her to their bed because he thought that would help him ease Finn into being with a man. Tonight was her last chance to help them do that.

She grinned as she considered the way she hoped the night would play out.

Walking down the hall, she enjoyed the way both men's eyes widened when she entered the living room naked.

"I don't remember telling you to get undressed," Finn said, using *that* tone.

"I figured it was inferred," she teased. Glancing over, she realized they'd turned off the TV. "Hockey game over?"

"You know it's not," Finn replied.

"Wow. You're picking me over hockey. You just scored mega brownie points."

While Miguel chuckled at her joke, Finn never cracked a smile, his gaze raking over her from head to toe. They'd seen her naked more than dressed this past week, and their approving appraisal never failed to make her hot.

"Sit in that chair."

She'd been so distracted, she hadn't realized they'd moved a cushioned armchair into the middle of the room, opposite the couch where they both still sat.

She sat down on the comfortable chair, placing the lube on the coffee table between her and her guys.

Miguel glanced at the lube. "I hardly think that's going to be necessary. Never known you not to be wet and ready to go."

"That's not for me," she said, lifting her eyebrows suggestively.

Miguel looked interested. Finn's expression only turned darker.

"What part of you're not running the show do you keep struggling with, LJ?"

Finn had told her the first night they were together, he and Miguel would call the shots. Not that it had stopped her from making countless suggestions over the past week.

Miguel was still looking at the lube. "I think maybe we should hear what Layla had in mind for the lube."

She giggled as Finn shot Miguel a look that said he'd pay for that later.

Finn shook his head. "No. Layla is obviously concerned about having to take care of her own needs after tonight. I think we owe it to her to make sure she's got a good handle on her masturbation skills."

Her cheeks heated, though she wasn't embarrassed. She loved the idea of using the vibrator on herself in front of them.

Finn gestured to the vibrator in her hand. "Show us your technique."

She wanted to put on a good show for them, wanted to make sure they were just as turned on by this as she intended to be. She turned the vibrator on low, placing the tip of it against one of her nipples. She'd never realized how much of an erogenous zone her nipples really were until Finn and Miguel. They were connoisseurs when it came to breast play.

Miguel leaned forward, his elbows on his knees, watching her intently.

Finn, however, remained relaxed, poised, though she knew he was just as enthralled, just as in tune with what she was doing.

After teasing both nipples with the vibrator, drawing them out until they were large and hard and erect, she cupped one breast. She was well-endowed enough that she could draw her own nipple into her mouth, a trick she hadn't shown the guys yet.

"Fuck," Miguel whispered as she sucked on her own tight nipple.

Finn's eyes narrowed with desire and he moved forward. She thought he was going to stand up and come to her, but at the last minute, he seemed to recall their purpose, and he leaned back once again.

"You've been holding out on us," he murmured darkly.

She grinned, releasing the nipple with a loud pop before drawing the vibrator over her breasts again, then lowering it over her stomach.

"Place your legs over the arms of the chair," Finn demanded.

She shot him an annoyed look. "Is this my show or yours?"

He didn't move, but there was something very alpha, very intimidating in his pose, when he said, "Now, Layla."

It was the first time he'd ever used her real name, eschewing her childhood nickname. Electricity shimmered over the surface of her skin, and she lifted her legs over the armrests, exposing herself fully to them.

"Tease your clit the same way you just did your nipples. Touch it with just the tip of the vibrator. On low."

Finn had assumed command, but Layla didn't bother to try to reclaim it. She wanted this, wanted him to exert his power over her. She loved it.

She touched her clit, her hips jerking at the stimulus. Her eyes closed in bliss.

"Open your eyes," Miguel said. "Don't take them off us."

As he spoke, he stood and shoved his pants off. Both men had changed out of their work clothes as soon as they got home, opting to spend the evening shirtless, wearing nothing but comfortable lounge pants. His cock was thick and hard. He wrapped his hand around it and stroked it a few times before sitting back down.

She licked her lips and considered calling the game off. She didn't think they'd put up much of a fuss if she slipped off the chair and crawled across the floor to kneel in front of them. What guy turned down a blowjob?

She was just about to make her move when Finn stopped her.

"Pay attention to what you're doing."

She'd gotten so distracted, she'd forgotten about her toy, the thing still vibrating on low in her lap. She lifted it again and placed it to her clit.

"God," she breathed. It felt so good, and she was so ready to be finished with this. She wanted Finn and Miguel, wanted the three of them to move this game to the bed, so they could bury themselves deep inside her.

She moved the vibrator to her opening and started to slide it in.

"I was afraid of that," Finn said, capturing her attention. "Too impatient. You're as bad as Miguel."

Miguel grinned unabashedly as he tightened his grip on his cock. "Just because you're a sadist, don't expect me to deny myself the pleasures of the flesh."

Finn reached over and closed his hand over Miguel's, halting his friend's stroking.

"Finn," Miguel said warningly, when it was clear Finn didn't intend to move his hand.

"You're going to get off tonight. But not by jacking off. Understand?"

Miguel blew out a long, slow breath, then released his grip on his cock. Finn smiled, then turned his attention back to her. Once again, she'd been so distracted by the interchange between Finn and Miguel, she'd forgotten the vibrator. It was only a few inches inside her, the low setting barely registering.

Finn shook his head and rose, walking over to her. "What am I going to do with the two of you?" There was something so affectionate, so...sweet about the way he asked the question, that her breath hitched and her heart panged.

"Fuck us?" she asked, unable to hold back her laughter. She was depressed as hell about ending this affair, but damn if she wasn't unbelievably happy at the moment. It felt like she could burst from the sheer joy inside her.

Finn broke, his stern alpha male persona vanishing as he laughed loudly. "Yeah. I think that's exactly what I'm going to have to do."

He perched himself on the side of the coffee table and took the vibrator from her hands. "Scoot your ass closer to the edge of the chair. You're not hot enough yet."

"You're kidding, right?"

Finn sobered quickly, raising one imperious eyebrow, not bothering to repeat himself.

She scooted. The second she was in position, Finn pushed her knees farther apart.

"Miguel," Finn said. "Come stand behind our girl. Play with those pretty tits of hers."

Miguel was behind her in a moment, his large hands cupping her firmly, pinching her nipples the way they both knew she loved.

"I want you to remember this the next time you pull out your vibrator. I want you to close your eyes and see this moment. Feel Miguel's hands on your breasts, his hot breath on your cheek, his lips on your neck." As he spoke, Miguel did everything Finn said. "I want you to hear my voice, and I want you to imagine that this toy is me, thrusting inside you. Taking you deep and hard." Finn's actions also mimicked his words as he pushed the vibrator in all the way to the hilt, his knuckles bumping against her clit until she saw stars. Her pussy clenched greedily when he turned the toy up to high.

"Oh my God," she cried out. Finn said he wanted her hot,

but he'd missed the mark by a mile. This wasn't merely hot, it was an inferno, a nuclear reaction. "I, God...I'm going to..."

The toy disappeared. At the worst fucking time.

Layla's eyes flew open, her orgasm-deprived brain trying to focus on what she was seeing. Finn had risen from the coffee table and he'd taken her salvation with him.

She trembled, her hands flying toward her clit. One touch. All she needed was one—

Miguel grasped her wrists firmly, holding her back.

"No!" she yelled.

Finn's voice was somewhere behind her, not as close as she wanted. "Bring her to the bedroom. And don't forget the lube."

Miguel helped her up, giving her a cocky grin when she stumbled on unsteady legs.

"Asshole," she murmured, though there was no heat behind the insult. They loved bringing her to this point, dragging her right to the edge of her climax, then retreating. She'd be more pissed off if she hadn't learned in the past seven days that Finn and Miguel always—*always*—made the wait worth it.

Miguel wrapped one arm around her waist, then bent to retrieve the lube. He kissed her on the cheek affectionately. "I love you too," he teased.

Layla knew he meant the words playfully, but they struck her more effectively than Cupid's arrow.

Love.

She loved him. Loved both of them.

What the hell was she supposed to do now?

$\mathcal{H}$  14  $\mathcal{H}$

Miguel held Layla tight as they walked down the hallway to the bedroom. He hoped she'd been too out of her mind to register his profession of love.

Not that the feelings weren't there. Fuck. He was head over heels in love with Layla.

But he hadn't intended to say that out loud. Especially considering that was the last thing she wanted from them.

*Casual sex.*

*No strings attached.*

He was seriously starting to hate those concepts.

When they entered his bedroom, Miguel stopped for a second to suck in some much-needed air. Finn had stripped off his pants and was waiting for them beside the bed. He'd pulled down the covers and positioned a couple of pillows in the middle of the mattress.

He loved the way Finn took control in the bedroom.

Fuck. There was that word again.

Love.

He took another steadying breath and decided to hell with it. He'd spent the better part of this year in love with his best friend, and there weren't too many people left who didn't know it. The problem was...he hadn't meant to fall so hard for Layla too.

"Come here, LJ." Finn crooked a finger at their girl and she went quickly. Too quickly.

He and Finn chuckled at her enthusiasm. She hadn't lied about her desire to experience it all in the bedroom. Hell, there were times when it felt like he and Finn were struggling to keep up with her, and they'd both put a few thousand miles on their mattresses in the past.

Finn took her hand, gently pushing her toward the bed. "Lay on your stomach and prop those pillows under your waist. I want your ass in the air."

Layla did exactly as he asked, and Miguel took a minute to admire her gorgeous ass. She was—hands down—the most beautiful woman he'd ever seen. He approached the bed and ran his hand over her soft skin, provoking a shiver.

He flashed a grin at Finn, but his best friend didn't return it. Instead, he was looking at Miguel with something that couldn't be called anything but desire.

Miguel fought to hold Finn's gaze, tried to stave off the light-headedness. It would be easier if every drop of blood in his body wasn't currently residing in his cock. He'd never been this hard, this ready.

"Get on the bed," Finn said, his voice gravelly with need. "Kneel behind LJ. You're going to fuck our girl while I fuck you."

"Holy shit," Layla breathed softly from the bed, her ass wiggling as if she couldn't contain her arousal.

Miguel held his breath for just a moment, waiting for Finn to reconsider, but there wasn't a drop of hesitance on his friend's face.

"You want me," Miguel said, no question to his words.

Finn gave him his standard easygoing, roguish smile, the one that told Miguel his friend was down for anything and everything.

All in.

"More than I can say, Miguel."

Miguel climbed onto the bed and shifted until he was kneeling between Layla's legs. He gripped his cock and ran the tip of it through her slit. She was wet and hot and too ready to go. She tried to move closer to him, tried to draw him inside, but he gripped her hips and held her still.

"Not yet, Brown Eyes," Miguel murmured, bending over her back so he could kiss her cheek, her ear, her hair. Then he glanced over his shoulder at Finn. "Want instructions?"

Finn laughed and shook his head. "No, you asshole. I think I can figure it out."

They all laughed. God. It was always so much fun with them. They got each other. On every level. Miguel hadn't had a best friend growing up, hadn't even had a group of friends. It had been simpler and safer to fly alone, to get through high school without succumbing to the lure of the gangs, and then get the fuck out of the Bronx.

Finn and Landon and the Collins family had been the first people to accept him for who he was, to include him in their ranks. And with Layla and Finn, Miguel felt safe to lower *all* the walls, to truly be himself. It was the most incredible feeling in the world.

Miguel was pulled back to the present when the mattress shifted and he felt the first few drops of lube hit his ass.

"Fuck," he whispered reverently. The chilliness lasted only a few seconds before Finn heated it up, pressing one finger all the way into his ass.

Miguel remained still over Layla as Finn worked a second finger in, stretching him. He'd spent a week looking at his best friend's dick. Finn was larger than his past lovers, not that Miguel had a problem with that. At all. Shit, he'd be lucky to hold off his climax through the first thrust. He was too fucking ready for this.

Layla lifted her ass, wiggling it against his cock. Miguel grinned. She was fighting some serious arousal of her own.

"Take it easy, baby," he soothed. "Soon." His last word ended with a groan when Finn withdrew briefly, returning with three fingers. "Shit. Yeah." He was stretched to the point of discomfort, but there was no way he was calling a halt.

Finn added more lube, slowed down, took his time. Miguel struggled to believe this was his friend's first time with a man. He knew everything to do.

"So good, Finn," Miguel murmured.

"It doesn't hurt?" It was the first time he'd heard the slightest bit of uncertainty from Finn.

Miguel looked over his shoulder. "Yeah. A little. But it's a good hurt. I'll show you one night."

Finn grinned. "We're going to have to work up to that, I'm afraid."

Miguel winked at his best friend—and now his lover. "We've got all the time in the world."

Finn nodded, then pressed all three fingers in to the hilt.

"Jesus." Miguel bent his head, his forehead pressed to Layla's back.

"I wish I could see what he's doing to you," she whispered to Miguel.

"Next time," he said, praying Layla wouldn't hold them to the time limit, wouldn't insist on ending things come morning. He didn't want this to end. Ever.

She didn't reply. Instead, she wiggled her ass against his cock once more, and Miguel fought every instinct that had him desperate to take exactly what she was offering. He wanted to push into that tight pussy of hers and fuck them both to oblivion.

But he wanted Finn with them.

"Finn," he said.

Finn must have heard the hunger, the need. He pulled his fingers out, and Miguel glanced over his shoulder, watching as Finn put on a condom and lubed it up. Then he reached around

Miguel's waist and slowly, torturously, rolled a condom onto his dick.

"Fuck. Me," Miguel breathed. This wasn't going to last five seconds. "You're killing me, bro."

"Don't come too fast, Miguel," Finn warned with a joking tone. "Or I'll give you shit for it for the rest of our lives."

Miguel started to laugh, even though he knew Finn was a man of his word. The two of them were masters of trash talking and Finn's threat did the trick, presented Miguel with a challenge he refused to lose.

Miguel lifted Layla's hips slightly and lined his cock up with her opening. She shuddered as he pressed inside.

"Finally," she said, her pussy clenching too tightly against him.

She wasn't going to make this easy on him.

"Layla. If you have an ounce of compassion inside you, you'll fight against that orgasm for a little while. Let it build slow. If you come, there's no way I—"

That was all Miguel managed to say before he felt the head of Finn's dick stretching his ass.

"Goddammit," Miguel said through gritted teeth.

"Fuck, man." Finn was only a few inches inside, but he stopped for a second. "This is...Jesus..." He pressed in another inch. And then another. Both of them groaning with desire, need and, in Miguel's case, just the slightest bit of pain.

"All of it, Finn. Give me *all* of it."

Finn didn't hesitate, didn't resist the invitation. He thrust in deeply, filling Miguel's ass. Then he withdrew and slid all the way back in. Finn set an easy pace at first, careful as he stretched his anus. On each inward thrust, Miguel's cock shifted deeper inside Layla, who picked up the rhythm quickly. She was there each time, pressing back against him, adding her own pressure, her own delicious torture.

Miguel lost track of time, of place, of everything. All he knew was what he felt, and all he felt was bliss, heaven. His heart raced and he wondered if his lovers could hear it pounding. Blood rushed through his ears, deafening him. He'd wanted Finn inside him for so long—a lifetime, it seemed. But he'd never let himself truly believe they'd get here.

Now, they were and Miguel knew he'd never recover from this. He was irrevocably changed—a man living his dream, who'd found his place in the world.

Right here.

With Finn.

With Layla.

"Harder," he managed to say after a few minutes.

Finn had apparently been waiting for him to wave that red flag. His friend tightened his grip on his hips and slammed deep, driving Miguel into Layla, who cried out.

"Oh God, Miguel," she said. "I can't...I'm sorry...I—"

Layla came. Hard. So fucking hard.

Miguel didn't have a snowball's chance in hell of resisting his own climax. His balls tightened, then exploded, filling the condom as lightning strike after lightning strike flashed through him. He yelled out Layla's name, then Finn's, over and over.

Finn was only half a minute behind him, coming loudly as well, his thrusts growing less controlled, more haphazard as he came roughly.

Miguel locked his elbows, fighting to hold himself up so he didn't crush Layla with his weight. Finn shifted, both of them groaning as he withdrew from Miguel's ass.

Finn left the bed and Miguel listened as his friend walked to the bathroom. He heard water running. He wished he could find the strength to do the same.

Layla pulled the pillows from beneath her and flipped over, even as Miguel caged her between this arms. She smiled up at him, lifting her hands to his shoulders. He lowered himself to her, pressing his chest to her breasts so that he could kiss her.

It was a long, soft kiss, both of them sated, happy. They

didn't break the union of their lips until they felt Finn's weight on the mattress next to them.

"Don't stop on my account," he said, running his hand over Miguel's back and ass. "I love watching the two of you kiss."

Miguel felt the same way, loved playing voyeur to Layla and Finn.

He forced himself up. "I need to clean up. Get rid of this condom." Miguel padded to the bathroom, glancing over his shoulder to watch as Finn lay down next to Layla and pulled her into his arms.

Love.

The word drifted through his mind again, the feeling more powerful than ever.

He loved them.

Both of them.

He stood in front of the bathroom mirror and studied his reflection, slightly surprised to see the same old face looking back.

He felt completely different, utterly changed.

And yet, he looked exactly the same.

He threw the condom away and splashed cold water on his face, grabbing a washcloth to clean up.

When he returned to the room, Finn and Layla were both sound asleep. He chuckled softly. They'd had quite a workout.

And while he was exhausted as well, he knew he wasn't going to be able to fall asleep as easily. There were too many thoughts racing through his brain, too many emotions coursing through him.

He knew without a shadow of a doubt what he wanted, but he wasn't sure how to broach the subject. After all, Layla wasn't looking for a boyfriend—or in this case, two—and he'd only just embarked on this new relationship with Finn.

Could he change the rules at this stage of the game without losing them both?

Miguel had never been a coward, never shied away from what he wanted.

Until Finn.

And now Layla.

And he realized why. In the past, his heart had never been engaged. He'd never felt the bone-shaking terror of losing the most important people in his life. He couldn't imagine living his life without either of them.

So...this was love.

Wow.

It sucked.

## 15

Finn sat in the corner booth at Pat's Pub, nursing his Guinness, ignoring the dinner rush, the constant ebb and flow of patrons coming and going. He knew most of the people in the place, but apparently he was wearing his miserable heart on his sleeve because, aside from a few hellos, everyone was giving him a wide berth.

He'd been sitting alone for the past two hours, trying to wrap his head around everything that had occurred last night. And this morning.

Talk about a life-changing twenty-four hours.

So many things had happened that he felt sort of numb.

He'd had sex with Miguel.

He'd fucked another man.

And holy shit, had he enjoyed it.

After that explosive sex, he'd fallen asleep, waking up in the wee hours of the night to discover he was spooning Layla. She must have felt him stir, because she'd pressed her rear end closer and he'd gotten hard. His permanent condition whenever he was with Layla and Miguel.

Drowsily, he'd kept his eyes closed as he'd pressed inside her, moving in and out slowly. Layla began to meet his thrusts, though neither of them sought to increase the pace, content to just savor the moment. She'd moaned softly when he'd shifted slightly and found her G-spot.

Then the bed shifted, and his eyelids had popped opened when he felt the covers being pulled down.

Miguel was on his side, facing them, propped up on one elbow. He'd lowered the covers in order to have a better view.

Finn gripped Layla's hip, pulling her toward him, over and over. After a few minutes, Miguel reached down, his fingers toying with Layla's clit. Then they drifted lower, lightly caressing Finn's cock as he shifted inside her.

Miguel had been more awake, more cognizant of what was going on because he'd been the one to point out they'd forgotten a condom. Finn had started to withdraw, but Layla stopped him, told them she was on birth control, that she didn't want anything between them.

After that, Finn was a goner. He took what she offered, making love to her, wishing—hoping—she could see what she meant to him. They came together.

Then he'd withdrawn and watched as Miguel moved over her, parted her legs and made love to her as well.

They'd fallen asleep in a tangle of limbs, none of them rousing until late this morning.

That was when the bottom fell out.

Layla had been fully dressed and sitting on the side of the bed when he and Miguel woke. She'd thanked them for the best week of her life.

Finn had wanted to beg her for more time, wanted to plead with her to stay, but he didn't.

He couldn't. Because of Miguel.

Like idiots, they hadn't discussed what would happen when the week ended. They'd been driven by their dicks.

Miguel hadn't tried to stop her either.

Instead, they'd kissed her goodbye, then Miguel had gotten up to shower for work.

Finn had dressed, yelled into the bathroom to tell Miguel he'd see him later and headed back to the Collins Dorm, fighting like mad not to break down and cry like a baby the whole way home.

"Padraig is threatening to charge you rent if you hog this table much longer."

Finn looked up and forced a grin as Colm sat down. "I'm a paying customer."

"Shit, seriously? I never pay for my drinks here," Colm joked. "What gives? Paddy says you've been nursing the same Guinness for two hours." To confirm that fact, Colm reached out and touched his glass. "Jesus. It's warm." He raised his hand to capture his twin brother's attention behind the bar. "Two more beers over here, Paddy. Put them on my tab," he added with a laugh.

Padraig came over with three beers and claimed the opposite side of the booth. "Oliver said he'd cover the bar for a few minutes. Pretty nice having that kid here and of age finally. Plan to take advantage of that more. I miss too many conversations that you bozos refuse to have at the bar. Thinking of taking the booths and tables out of the pub completely so I stop missing all the good gossip."

"You're getting as nosy as Pop Pop," Finn said.

"If that's meant to be an insult, you missed the mark." Padraig loved being likened to their beloved grandfather, took any and all comparisons as compliments. Then he glanced over his shoulder and grinned. "Emmy is going to be pissed that we've moved out of earshot."

Colm rolled his eyes. "Just ask her out already, Paddy. You're into her, and she's into you."

Padraig sobered and shook his head. "No. I'm not...I don't think...I'm not looking to date anyone."

Finn nodded in understanding, while Colm simply looked sad. Mia had been gone two years, and Padraig had given no indication that he'd ever be ready. Sometimes it felt as if Padraig had died with her, and Finn knew it worried the hell out of his brother.

"You're not looking to date anyone *yet*," Colm amended, proving he didn't intend to give up on pressing the issue.

Padraig shrugged, letting his determined twin have the last word. "My love life isn't in question at the moment. It's Finn's."

"What makes you think anything's wrong with my love life?"

Padraig took a sip of his Guinness, then lowered the glass. "The last time we talked, you were mooning over Layla. And I have it on very good authority, you haven't spent a single night in your bed this week."

"Let me guess," Finn said, looking at Colm. "You're the good authority."

Colm nodded, not bothering to feign the slightest bit of regret. "Yup."

"Snitches get stitches," Finn joked.

"So, I have deducted," Colm said, in his best lawyer voice, "that you've been shacking up with the pretty Ms. Moretti."

Colm wasn't wrong, but he only had half the facts. Finn leaned back and debated whether or not to come clean about all of it.

Fuck it. His cousins were like brothers to him, and he needed advice.

"Not just LJ."

Apparently, his depression wasn't so deep that he couldn't enjoy the matching looks of surprise on Colm's and Padraig's faces.

Padraig was the first to put two and two together, and his smile grew. "Miguel."

Finn nodded.

"About time. Just tell me you did it right," Colm said, leaning closer. "Tell me the two of you didn't take the coward's way out and pretend you were only there for Layla."

"We didn't."

"So you and Miguel..." Colm prodded with a wicked grin.

Finn rolled his eyes. "I'm not giving you the details."

Colm laughed and slapped Finn on the shoulder. "Don't need them. Just glad to hear there are some details to be had."

The weight that had been pressing on Finn's chest since this morning lifted a little. Not a lot, but there'd been a part of him—a foolish part—that had sort of worried how his family would take the news that he and Miguel were sleeping together. He should have—and had—expected this reaction. After all, their uncles, Sean and Chad, had been together for decades, the two men lovers, married to each other and Aunt Lauren.

Besides, it wasn't as if he and Miguel had hidden their feelings particularly well. Even Pop Pop had noticed the sexual undercurrents flowing between them.

"So, the three of you spent the past week together. Sounds pretty perfect considering you have feelings for both of them." Padraig always saw right to the heart of things. "Unless...let me guess...Layla is finished sowing her wild oats with the two of you."

Finn couldn't bring himself to admit that truth. Because he couldn't accept it.

"Wild oats?" Colm asked.

Mercifully, Padraig took up the explanation. Finn's throat was suddenly constricted as he considered perhaps Layla really was moving on from them. "Layla just got out of a long relationship. She's resistant to hopping into another. Apparently, she moved to Baltimore for a fresh start that includes casual sex and one-night stands."

"You lucky son of a bitch," Colm, the eternal bachelor, mused. "Why can't I ever meet women like that? Last two women I took out were ready to go ring shopping three dates in."

"I'm living for the day love bites you in the ass," Padraig said, the comment one Finn had heard countless times over the years, before turning his attention back to Finn. "Thought I'd suggested that you convince her otherwise."

"You did. It's just..."

Colm frowned. "Miguel doesn't want to share?"

"I don't know."

Padraig had been about to take another sip of beer, but he lowered his pint glass. "What do you mean you don't know?"

"I mean I didn't ask what he wanted."

"Why not?" Colm asked.

Finn found everything that had been eating him alive over the past week falling out. "Because I've only just come clean about my feelings for Miguel. To him and myself. Because I've hurt him these past couple of months, pushing him away because I couldn't face what was happening between us. Because I'm in love with him. Don't I owe it to him to try to make this thing between us work...with just *us*?"

"I'd say yes," Padraig began, "if not for the other half of the story. You're in love with someone else too."

"Someone who's not looking for love."

"That hardly changes your feelings for her," Colm pointed out. "And it doesn't explain why you wouldn't tell Miguel you love her."

"We didn't intend for this affair to last long. In fact, Miguel was the one who set the time limit. One week. He only asked for one week."

"And that ended today?" Padraig asked.

Finn nodded miserably. "LJ held us to it. Said goodbye this morning, and Miguel didn't argue. So I let her go. I didn't stop her because..."

Padraig sighed. "Because you don't want to hurt Miguel if he doesn't feel the same way you do."

"I've hurt him enough."

Colm placed a comforting hand on his shoulder. "That hardly matters at this point. Because now *you're* hurting. What do you want from this, Finn? Choose your best-case scenario. How do you want this to play out?"

The answer flew out in an instant. Finn didn't even have to think about it. "I want them both. Forever."

Colm laughed. "You always were a greedy bastard."

"Then make it happen." Padraig acted as if achieving that goal was the easiest thing on the planet.

"Paddy—" Finn started.

"You've got Collins blood running through your veins. Trust me. There's nothing we can't do once we've set our minds to it. If you love both of them, find a way. We've all seen firsthand that three can love and live happily ever after as easily as two. Don't give up without trying."

Finn smiled...and felt the first ray of hope emerge since watching Layla walk away from him and Miguel this morning.

"That was a hell of a pep talk," he said to Padraig.

"Call Miguel. Start there," Padraig said.

"He's working tonight. The robbery case is really kicking his ass, and I don't want to distract him. Besides, this is a conversation we need to have in person. I'll go see him first thing in the morning."

Padraig patted his hand and stood up, glancing toward the bar. "Better get back to work. Emmy and Ollie—oh, and Pop Pop—will be chomping at the bit for details."

Finn turned his attention to the bar and, sure enough, he spotted Pop Pop—who'd just arrived—as well as Emmy and Oliver, all looking at them. The three of them turned their heads away quickly when they saw Finn looking, and he laughed.

Padraig returned to the bar.

Finn shook his head. "Something tells me Pop Pop, Paddy and Emmy are not going to be a good influence on Oliver."

Colm considered that. "Always figured it would be you and me working together, trying to save the boy."

"What do you mean?" Finn asked.

"Not going to lie," Colm said, "I thought you and I had the best shot at dodging the curse. Turns out it got you twice. Fucking thing is tenacious."

"Comforting, Colm," Finn said sarcastically. "Very comforting. You realize no part of my future is solid, and if things don't work out..."

Colm chuckled. "They'll work out. On top of being greedy, you're a stubborn bastard. I figure you get that from your mom. Aunt Riley has never heard the word no."

Finn couldn't help but laugh as well. His family was the best when it came to cheering him up.

"Hey, guys," Darcy said, approaching the table. "What's shakin'?"

"What are you all dressed up for? Got a hot date?" Colm asked.

Darcy shook her head. "Something even better. Girls' night out. Meeting Kelli and Layla downtown. Three single ladies on the prowl."

Finn scowled at his little sister, ready to tell her she wasn't going anywhere, then he forced himself to calm down. Darcy didn't know about his feelings for Layla. As far as she knew, the two of them were still hanging out in the friend zone, so it wasn't like she realized what her plans were doing to him at the moment.

Colm nudged him under the table with his knee.

"Not sure I like you hanging out with Kelli. She's a bad influence," Colm said, trying to distract Finn.

Darcy laughed. "Bullshit. She's the best kind of influence, and you know it."

Colm and Kelli had some sort of love/hate relationship that no one in the family understood. Basically, they loved to hate each other and constantly gave each other shit.

"Where are you going?" Finn asked, trying and failing to sound nonchalant.

Darcy shrugged. "No idea. The plan is to barhop until we drop. Or at least that was what Layla said when she called to invite me."

"This was LJ's idea?" This time Finn completely showed his

hand, unable to hide his anger.

Darcy tilted her head as she studied his face. "Um...yeah? Did something happen between you two?"

Finn shook his head, then rubbed his forehead wearily. Layla hadn't wasted any time moving on. He took a deep breath and somehow managed to control his features. "No," he lied.

"You okay, Finn?" Darcy asked.

"Yeah. I'm great." He was working overtime to sound like he didn't have a care in the world.

"Okay. Are you sure?" she asked again, because his astute sister wasn't buying his lies.

He nodded.

Darcy didn't believe him, but mercifully she didn't keep questioning him either. Mainly because she had other tricks up her sleeve. "Well, I guess I'll head out. Don't wait up. We're probably going to get back super late. If we even come home at all," she said with a mischievous smile.

She was testing him, waiting to see if he lost his shit. Typical of his kid sisters. Darcy, the baby of the family, had studied under Sunnie, so she'd learned from the master. She knew something was up, and since he wasn't coming clean, she was trying to provoke a response.

Colm's knee nudged him under the table again, silently telling him to hold it together.

"I have you on Find My Friends, Darc. I'm perfectly capable of keeping an eye on you." Finn had been following his sisters on the app for years. In this day and age—with sex trafficking and catfishing on online dating sites, he and their dad had convinced them it was smart to allow Finn to track them on their phones. Finn had promised to never use the app against them, and he never had. Tonight, he wasn't so sure he'd be able to resist.

"I could always unshare my location," she taunted.

"Don't."

Darcy was taken aback by the pure malice in his voice. He

knew he was acting out of character, was showing his sister a side of him he didn't typically reveal.

When she didn't reply, he pushed the issue. "Promise me you won't."

"What's going on with you and Layla?"

"Nothing." Sadly, that wasn't a lie. Layla had said her good-byes to him and Miguel this morning, and neither of them harbored any illusions that she wouldn't move on with her life.

He just hadn't expected her to do it the same fucking night.

"I don't believe you, but I'm late. So I'm letting you off the hook for now. You can track me all night if you want. But tomorrow, I'm going to want some answers, okay?"

He nodded. For all their arguing, he and his sisters were close —friends as well as siblings. Hell, maybe Darcy could help him figure out how to convince Layla to...

To what?

The image of Miguel's face flashed through his mind.

Fuck.

"We'll talk tomorrow."

Darcy gave him a quick peck on the cheek. "Love you, big bro."

He forced a smile and watched as she sashayed out of the bar in her too-short skirt and a shirt that revealed at least two inches of her stomach. God help him if Layla was dressed similarly.

He wasn't sleeping tonight. No doubt, he'd have his phone in hand all night, constantly refreshing the app, following his little sister *and* Layla throughout the city.

## 16

I t took a lot of effort for Layla to smile at the guy as she excused herself and walked off the dance floor. Kelli and Darcy were standing by the table they were sharing, scream-talking to each other. The music in the club was one decibel away from deafening.

Darcy handed her a full drink when she made her way back to them. "Your dance partner bought you another drink," Darcy yelled.

Layla grimaced. This was the third drink the guy had sent to her. It was obvious he was expecting to get lucky, but there was no way in hell she was leaving this club with him. The guy—shit, she couldn't even remember his name—was seriously starting to annoy her.

Not that it was really his fault. He was actually a pretty nice guy. He just...wasn't Finn or Miguel. Something that was driven home when he'd kissed her at the end of the last song. The kiss hadn't lasted more than a few seconds, and it wasn't particularly bad. It just hadn't done a damn thing for her.

Worse than that, it had turned her off, left her cold inside.

There was no question the guy was more than willing to

expand on the kiss later at her place. All she had to do was issue the invitation.

Which she was not going to do.

So much for expanding her sexual horizons and casual hookups. Just the thought of sleeping with a stranger made her stomach turn.

What the hell had she been thinking?

She wasn't a one-night stand girl.

She was a one-man woman. Or, well, maybe a two-man woman.

"Hey."

She looked up and inwardly groaned. No Name was back.

"I didn't have a chance to eat dinner tonight. Thought I might head out for a burger. You wanna come?"

Layla glanced at Kelli and Darcy, who clearly hadn't heard him issue the invitation over the music. Layla shook her head. "No thanks. I'm getting a headache from the noise in here. I think I might go home."

Mr. What the Hell is His Name looked hopeful. "Want some company?"

Fuck. How had that sounded like an invitation? "I really don't feel well," she stressed.

"Can I call you sometime?"

She didn't want to give this guy her number, didn't want to lead him on. She shook her head. "I don't think this is going to work out. I just got out of a relationship and..."

The guy nodded and gave her a friendly smile. "No problem. I understand. Maybe I'll see you around."

Now she felt even more terrible. He was a decent guy, but when he'd kissed her on the dance floor, it had driven home just how fucked up she was.

Her stomach hurt, her chest was tight, her heart ached.

Shit. She hadn't been this devastated over Marco and they'd dated for five years.

"You guys want to get out of here?" Layla shouted over the

music. Both Kelli and Darcy looked thrilled by the prospect of leaving.

"Hell yeah," Kelli shouted back. "I can't hear myself think in here."

They settled up their tab then left the club, stopping on the sidewalk.

Layla tried to unplug her ears with her fingers. "I think I have permanent hearing damage."

Darcy laughed and nodded. "That was insanely loud."

Kelli looked at the time on her phone. "You know it's still early."

It was. Layla had really built the night up in her invitation, billed it as the ultimate GNO. They'd only been in the one club, but she couldn't face the prospect of hitting another.

"At the risk of sounding old," Kelli began. "How would you two feel about blowing off the club scene and grabbing a glass of wine at a very quiet restaurant somewhere on the waterfront?"

"Sounds perfect," Darcy said.

"Oh thank God. I'm in." Layla was grateful neither of the other women wanted to hit another club. She'd invited them out this afternoon after spending the entire morning crying over Miguel and Finn. Like a jackass, she'd thought the best cure for her woes was to immediately get back on the horse.

Now, she was starting to think she'd never ride again.

Kelli called for an Uber and they continued to chat about the meat market they'd just escaped. Once they were settled at a quiet table at a restaurant on the waterfront, wine in hand, Kelli asked, "So what's the deal with you and Finn?"

Layla looked at Kelli, wondering what the other woman had heard. "What makes you think there's something between us?"

"A little birdie tells me that Finn hasn't been sleeping at home this week," Kelli said.

Layla looked at Darcy. "I suppose you're the little bird."

"Tweet tweet," Darcy said, grinning widely. "Let's just say I put two and two together. Finn's bed has been empty for a week, and given the grumpy ass I left in the pub earlier paired with your last-minute invitation to barhop, I figure something had to have happened."

In all of Darcy's deductions, there was one name left out. Miguel's. Which meant Finn's little sister didn't know the whole story. And there was no way Layla was going to fill her in on that. That wasn't her story to tell, and "coming out" for a guy to his family would be the ultimate dick move.

So she'd have to give these two women, whom she genuinely liked, half of the truth.

"We sort of detoured out of the friend zone," she said.

Both Darcy and Kelli looked too pleased, and Layla realized this was going to be harder than she thought. She could practically see the matchmaker in each of them emerging. Which meant Layla was going to have to come up with a lie about why things between her and Finn wouldn't work.

"And?" Kelli prompted.

"It was nice." Mind-blowing. Amazing. The most incredible experience of her life.

Darcy turned up her nose. "Nice? Sounds boring."

Layla needed to backtrack, lest she give Finn a bad reputation. "It was great, but..." She recalled her original reason for not entering into a relationship with Finn, and decided that was probably her best way to go. "But I've just gotten out of a long-term relationship and I'm not looking to jump right back into another one. I want to play the field, not tie myself down. Embrace my slutty side," she added, attempting humor.

"If that's true, then why did you send that guy back at the club packing?" Kelli asked. "He was more than willing to play with you."

"I wasn't attracted to him."

Darcy tilted her head. There was no denying she wasn't buying what Layla was shoveling. "I thought that guy was pretty cute and nice."

He was. He just wasn't Finn or Miguel.

"I'm playing the field," she said. "But I plan to be choosy, not promiscuous."

Kelli laughed. "Feels like someone needs the word *slut* defined for her."

Layla was in over her head with these two, which told her with any luck, they were about to become her best girlfriends. They weren't letting her get away with shit, and if she wasn't so fucking depressed, she'd love the hell out of them for that. "I just...wasn't interested in that guy," she said weakly.

"Can I give you a little advice?" Kelli asked, not bothering to wait for permission to impart her words of wisdom. "When you find the guy who rocks your world in bed, hold on to him. Trust me when I say, there are way more duds than studs in the world. Take it from the eternal bachelorette, playing the field sucks."

Darcy turned to look at Kelli in surprise. "I never knew you felt that way. Thought you enjoyed your single status."

Kelli shrugged. "Lately, I'm thinking I'd like to settle down. Have kids."

Darcy's eyes widened. "You've sworn off kids your whole life."

Kelli was a kindergarten teacher, so Layla was surprised to hear she wouldn't want some of her own. She must clearly like kids to be in that profession.

"I swore them off because after you've taught a few years, you realize it's going to be impossible to name a kid of your own because every name in the universe has been tarnished by some little shit in your classroom."

Layla laughed. "Why do I get the feeling you're a great teacher?"

Kelli took a sip of her wine. "I love my students. Love my job. And for a while, I loved my freedom. I don't feel that way anymore. I'm allowed to change my mind."

Darcy nodded. "You're right. You are. If you want a relationship, I'm all in on helping you find a guy. Layla will help, won't you?" she asked, turning back to her.

"Absolutely. I have four brothers I'll give you for free. You don't even have to pick one. You can just have all four."

Kelli pretended to consider that. "An Italian stallion harem. I could go for that. Tell the Moretti boys to give me a call."

Darcy laughed. "Or maybe you could coax Paddy back out into the world." It was obvious Darcy was worried about her cousin.

Kelli shook her head, covering Darcy's hand with hers and giving it a squeeze. "That's not going to be me, Darc. Paddy is my best friend. Being with him would be like being with a brother. And besides, he's not ready yet."

Darcy didn't look like she agreed.

"How about Colm, then?" Layla suggested.

Kelli scowled. "Jesus. I'd just as soon fuck Hans Gruber, Voldemort and Magneto."

"Wow. I didn't realize you and Colm got along so well," Layla joked.

Darcy rolled her eyes. "Let's just say Kelli and Colm don't see eye to eye on things."

"What sort of things?" Layla asked.

"Basically, everything. In the entire world." Darcy giggled.

Kelli flipped a long blonde curl over her shoulder. "That's putting it mildly. He's a womanizer and a chauvinist and the eternal man-child."

"I don't think he's a chauvinist," Darcy interjected.

Kelli laughed. "But you have no problem with the other two descriptions."

Darcy merely winked in reply. "What about Leo's roommate, Ryder?"

Kelli made a buzzer sound. "Errrr. Nice try, but I wasn't born yesterday and you're not fooling anyone. You've had a crush on that guy for years."

"No, I haven't."

Darcy's denial came way too quickly, and while Layla had no

idea who Ryder was, there was no doubt Kelli knew what she was talking about.

"Nice call, Kell," Layla said. "I'd say you hit that nail on the head."

"I'm kind of brilliant," Kelli deadpanned.

"I have no feelings for Ryder," Darcy persisted. "And even if I did, it would be pointless because he views me as too young. I'm the babysitter, for God's sake."

Kelli quickly filled Layla in on who Ryder was, explaining that, like Padraig, he'd lost his wife at a young age, the woman dying in a car accident. She'd left him alone to raise two sons—though one of the boys was a stepson. Apparently, Ryder and the other father, Leo, had decided to move in together to raise their sons so the brothers wouldn't have to be separated.

"I think that's the coolest story I've ever heard," Layla said. "Leo is the guy Yvonne just moved in with, right?"

Kelli nodded. "They're the freaking Brady Bunch. Yvonne and Leo, Ryder and the boys. And, of course, Darcy, the hot babysitter."

"Remind me why I hang out with you again," Darcy said.

"Because I'm fucking hilarious."

Layla laughed. Kelli cussed like a sailor, drank like a fish, was irreverent, a straight shooter, and so far from how she'd imagined a kindergarten teacher would be, it was crazy.

She'd invited these women out because she'd thought they'd all hit the clubs, she'd find some guy to distract her from her broken heart and, in doing so, find a way to avoid crying and eating Ben and Jerry's on her couch all night.

Instead, she'd gotten something much better. New friends who'd found a way to make her laugh.

"So, back to Layla," Darcy said, clearly ready to get off the subject of Ryder. "What are you going to do about Finn?"

Layla shrugged. Because that was the twenty-thousand-dollar question. "Don't worry about me. I'll figure it out," she lied, hoping it would appease the two women. It did.

They continued to talk for hours, as Darcy and Kelli told tale after tale about the Collins family, then listening as Layla shared about her papa and her crazy brothers.

She was actually smiling when she entered her apartment, well after midnight, but that faded fast when she recalled Darcy's question.

What was she going to do about Finn?

And Miguel?

What *could* she do?

She sighed when no answer came.

The only thing she knew was what she *couldn't* do.

One-night stands. Casual sex. No holds barred.

Because she'd done the one thing she swore she didn't want to.

She'd fallen in love.

## 17

Miguel rubbed his eyes as he stared at his computer screen. He wasn't seeing a damn thing on it, even though he was supposed to finish filling in his report. The masked robber—Darth Vader—had struck again. The guy was reusing the masks, not bothering to change characters anymore.

And because Miguel was avoiding real life, reluctant to return to his apartment—his bed—without Finn or Layla, he'd worked round the clock, determined to succeed at one fucking thing in his life. He wanted to catch the son of a bitch, so he'd been here twenty-four hours, first on the scene and, after that, glued to his office chair. He had the numb-as-fuck ass to prove it.

Finn had called a few minutes earlier to see if he wanted to meet for dinner tonight at the pub. Miguel had bailed, blaming work.

Finn told him that Layla had gone out with Darcy and Kelli last night. Miguel had tried to read Finn's tone, tried to decide if it was jealousy he'd heard in his best friend's voice or if he'd only imagined it because that was what *he* felt.

Then he wondered if Finn had dropped that little nugget as

his way of letting Miguel know Layla had moved on, and they could concentrate on their own relationship.

Miguel rested his elbow on his desk, cupped his forehead to hold it up. He was wiped out.

For a moment, he considered calling Finn back and taking him up on his offer to meet for dinner, but thought better of it. If he was a smart man, he'd clock out, head home and sleep for the next twelve hours.

But he couldn't do it. Couldn't face that empty bed.

He'd spent the better part of the day reliving every second with Layla and Finn. A few times, he'd tried to imagine sex with just Finn, but somehow, Layla always managed to sneak into the fantasy.

He was frustrated as hell. And confused.

Dammit. This was the last time he was going to make any decision based on his dick. Because now, in addition to being head over heels in love with Finn, he'd fallen pretty hard for Layla, who had no intention of dating either him *or* Finn.

"Garcia, my office. Now."

He looked up to see Aaron, Finn's father, glowering at him from his office doorway. As Miguel rose, Aaron stormed back inside to wait for him.

Great. This couldn't be good. Aaron was mild-mannered and easygoing, attributes he'd passed on to his son. His tone told Miguel this wasn't going to be a fun conversation.

His partner, Landon, gave him a supportive, if confused, look. The two of them hadn't worked together much the past few weeks, Miguel focusing on the rash of robberies as Landon did undercover work with the drug task force.

"Everything okay?" Landon murmured.

"Guess I'm about to find out."

"Yell if you need backup. Figure between the two of us, we can take the guy down."

Miguel laughed. Landon was probably the only guy on the force who wouldn't get killed by Aaron for providing backup in this situation. Primarily because Landon was married to Aaron's daughter, Sunnie. There were some perks to being the lieutenant's son-in-law.

"I think I can handle it." Miguel didn't think that at all, but he wasn't going to drag Landon into the mess he'd made. Mainly because Landon would be no help. The guy was still a newlywed, which meant he was well-laid and looking at the world through Sunnie-colored glasses.

Miguel walked into Aaron's office. He'd only made it two steps inside when Aaron jerked his head toward the door.

"Shut that," his boss demanded.

Miguel closed the door, then took the seat in front of Aaron's desk. "What can I do for you, sir?"

"Do you think you're going to pull your head out of your ass anytime soon or is it permanently stuck there?"

"Sir, if you're talking about the robbery case, I can promise you we're following every lead. I've just spent the last twelve hours—"

"I'm not talking about the robbery."

Miguel swallowed heavily. It would be a lot easier to take an ass-chewing for not closing a case than talking about anything personal. Aaron was his boss, and Finn...Finn was the boss's son.

"I'm not sure what—"

"I know about you and Finn."

Finn's family didn't function like the rest of the world. They took things like homosexuality and threesome marriages in stride. Live and let live, Finn had always said. It was one of the main things that had drawn him to Finn and his family. Most straight guys tended to build a wall after hearing Miguel was bi. Some of them probably didn't even realize they were doing it, but Miguel could always feel the new distance, always felt as if he was being held at arm's length.

He'd never felt that with Finn or the Collins family. He'd told them he was bi and they'd acted as if he'd said he had brown eyes or was left-handed. It hadn't made one bit of difference.

In the meantime, his uncle and mother were still struggling with his sexuality, and he'd taken care not to throw it in their faces. Not that they'd disowned him or even expressed outright disapproval. They were both old-fashioned, raised devout Catholics, and while it was hard for them to understand, they were trying.

Miguel loved them both with all his heart, and because of that, he'd shielded them from the things that made them uncomfortable, only introducing them to the girls he was dating, never the guys.

This time, he wanted to introduce them to Layla *and* Finn. But he wasn't going to pretend that would be an easy visit, and he didn't have a lot of confidence it would end well. It was one thing to like sleeping with men *and* women. It was another to do it at the same time.

"He told you?" Miguel asked, though he wasn't surprised.

Aaron shook his head. "No. He told Colm and Padraig, who told Pop, who told Riley, who told me first thing this morning."

Miguel rubbed his eyes wearily. "Excuse me for saying so, but your family is fucked-up."

Aaron laughed. "I'm related through marriage."

Maybe that was so, but it didn't mean his boss didn't fit with the Collins perfectly.

"I stopped by the pub on the way to work today and talked to Finn for a few minutes," Aaron said, not giving him a single clue what was said between them.

When the silence stretched and Miguel realized Aaron wasn't going to fill him in, he asked, "You okay with me and...Finn?"

Aaron nodded. "Not a question of how I feel—though for the record, of course I'm fine with it. Why wouldn't I be? You and Finn are good friends. But more than that, you bring out the best in each other."

Miguel smiled and realized at exactly that moment how much Aaron's approval mattered to him. "Thanks."

"It's how *you* feel that counts. And given the misery I've been witnessing the last twenty-four hours, I'd say you are not okay."

"How much did Finn tell you?" Miguel asked.

"All of it."

"So you know about Layla?"

Aaron nodded.

"None of this was planned, sir. Finn and I have been dancing around each other for a while. I knew he was straight, so I kept my distance. Or...I tried to. Then Layla moved back to Baltimore, and all of a sudden, Finn's spending all his time with this old friend, LJ. And I was okay with that because I thought LJ was a guy and Finn was straight. I met Layla when her coffee shop got robbed."

Aaron nodded. He knew Layla's place had been robbed. Knew about all the local businesses that had been hit.

"The two of us went out one night—Finn was in Vegas at that conference—and it was great. She's really cool. Layla was the first person to make me think that maybe I could get over my feelings for Finn. Then, I saw him kissing her at Pat's Pub a week or so ago. I lost my shit. Stormed out. Finn followed me and...I kissed him. And he kissed me back."

Aaron smiled. "Then what?"

Miguel ran his hand through his hair. "Layla followed us. Said it was the hottest kiss she'd ever seen. She thought...she saw the kiss and thought..."

"Thought the two of you were a couple," Aaron finished.

Miguel couldn't believe he was telling Aaron all of this, couldn't believe he was baring his soul to Finn's father, for God's sake. But the hard truth was, Miguel didn't have a father, and he couldn't share this with his uncle. And he didn't have a million cousins like Finn, who'd chosen to confide in Colm and Padraig and his dad. It also didn't help that he was running on fumes, that he was approaching the thirty-six-hour mark without sleep.

"Go on, son," Aaron encouraged. "What happened then?"

*Son.* That sounded nice.

Miguel shook that thought away and continued, "We told her we weren't a couple, but she'd seen that kiss. She saw how we felt about each other. So she told us to do it again. We didn't, we couldn't. And then, I sort of lost my mind and said the three of us needed to sleep together."

"What did Layla say to that?"

"She was all in. Finn was the harder one to convince."

Aaron chuckled. "Jesus. Sounds like you boys have found yourself a woman who approaches life the same way as Riley. You'll have a hell of a lot of fun, but God help you both."

Miguel laughed. Hard. Loud. And Aaron joined him.

Then reality snuck back in and Miguel sobered up. They'd found her. And lost her.

Aaron leaned toward him, his elbows on his desk. "So let's fast-forward. Because I don't need the locker-room version. Why are you and Finn both looking like you lost your best friend and your girl?"

Finn was upset too?

"We convinced Layla to give us a week. She just got out of a long relationship, and she's bound and determined not to tie herself down again."

Aaron sighed. "I'm assuming she held you to the one-week time limit."

Miguel nodded miserably. "She left us yesterday morning, wished us luck as a couple and walked out. According to Finn, she and Darcy and Kelli went barhopping last night."

"You and Finn going to try to be a couple?"

"I'm crazy about your son, sir. But whenever I think about us, about our future..."

"You want Layla there with you."

Miguel nodded.

"What's Finn want?"

"We haven't exactly talked about it."

Aaron closed his eyes and squeezed the top of his nose as if he was warding off a headache. "Miguel—" he started.

"In my defense," Miguel interjected, "there was another robbery and I've been working pretty much nonstop."

"I admire your dedication to your job." Aaron's tone was infused with enough sarcasm to let Miguel know that line was a crock of shit. "So I return to my first question. Are you going to pull your head out of your ass anytime soon? Call my idiot son, tell him how you feel, and then the two of you figure out how you're going to get the girl."

Miguel stood up, wishing he'd managed to be a bit steadier on his feet.

"But before you do that, go home. Sleep a few hours, then shower and shave. You look like shit." Aaron walked to the door of his office and opened it. "Landon," he called out. "Drive Garcia home."

"My bike's outside."

Aaron placed a fatherly hand on his shoulder. "You're exhausted. Do as I say and have some faith, Miguel. It'll all work out. Okay?"

Miguel nodded gratefully. "Thank you, sir."

"I think it's time for you to start calling me Aaron."

"That's going to be weird," Miguel joked.

"Tell me about it."

In the end, Miguel followed Aaron's instructions to the letter. He let Landon drive him home, he took a four-hour power nap, showered, shaved and headed to the pub. It was after eleven when he arrived, but the place didn't close until midnight. He glanced around the pub, then waved at Padraig behind the bar. It was a slow night, only a few patrons in the place.

"Finn?" he asked.

Padraig pointed above his head. "Dorm."

Miguel waved in thanks and headed toward the stairs at the back to the pub, the ones that led up to the apartment.

He grinned when he reached the top of the stairs. Oliver and Gavin were sitting on opposite sides of the coffee table, fists white knuckled as they faced off in one hell of an arm wrestling match. Darcy and Finn were sitting on the couch, cheering them on. Considering they were both cheering for a different guy, it was clear a wager had been placed.

Darcy brightened up when she saw him, rising to cross the room for a hug. "Miguel! Where the hell have you been? I swear it feels like I haven't seen you in ages."

As he looked around the apartment, he realized he felt the same. Over the past year, he'd spent as much time, if not more, at the Collins Dorm than his own place.

"Your dad's been kicking my ass at the precinct," he joked before pointing at Oliver and Gavin, still locked in mortal combat. "Who's your money on?"

"Gavin," she said. "Five bucks."

Finn hadn't risen from the couch, but Miguel had felt his friend's gaze on him since he'd entered the living room.

"You got a minute, Finn?" Miguel asked.

Finn nodded and stood up.

"What about the contest?" Oliver asked through gritted teeth.

He shouldn't have expended the effort. Gavin slammed his fist to the table, shouting victoriously.

"Dammit!" Oliver said. "Finn distracted me."

"Which is exactly why my money was on Gavin. You have the attention span of a toddler, Ollie," Darcy teased, holding her hand out as Finn slapped the five-dollar bill in her hand.

Finn's lack of bitching should have been a clue to the rest of them that something was up, but Darcy, Gavin and Oliver all settled back on the couch, pushing play on the movie they'd paused, the one that had obviously prompted the contest.

"*Over the Top*? Seriously?" Miguel asked.

Finn smirked. "The boys here are woefully ignorant on Stallone. I'm addressing some holes in their education. Come on. We'll head up to my room. I've seen this movie too many times to admit."

When they reached Finn's room, Finn closed the door

behind them as Miguel took a steadying breath before turning to face his best friend.

Finn didn't give him a chance to speak. Instead, he stepped right up to him and gave him a quick, hard, intense kiss.

"You're getting good at that," Miguel teased.

Finn shrugged then dropped down onto the side of his bed. "What can I say? I'm a lover, not a fighter."

"That would explain why you're shit at takedowns. Layla even got the better of you."

Finn rolled his eyes. "I let her take me down. Wanted to build up her confidence."

"Mmm-hmm. Is that what you're doing with me and Fergus every week?"

"You're a cop. He's ex-military. I'm bringing Ollie and Gavin next week to even out the playing field. Let you see what I can do when the cards are more evenly stacked."

"Might be fun with Oliver and Gavin there." Miguel dragged Finn's chair away from the desk, opting to sit there rather than the bed. He didn't trust himself to say what he needed to say if he and Finn were on the bed together.

If Finn thought his choice of seating was weird, he didn't let on.

"I'm glad you stopped by. I was hoping we could talk over dinner."

Miguel gave him a guilty grin. "Sorry for putting you off."

"It's okay. I know work's been crazy for you."

It wasn't work that had kept him away tonight. "Did Darcy say how her girls' night out with Layla and Kelli went?"

Finn shook his head. "Couldn't really bring myself to ask her. And because Darcy is Darcy, she offered nothing. She's going to make me ask before she'll give up anything. You're lucky you never had sisters, man. Both of mine live to torment me."

Miguel chuckled, agreeing that Finn's sisters loved to give him a hard time. But he also knew Sunnie and Darcy adored their big brother, and there were times when they looked at him like the sun rose and set on his shoulders. Miguel wouldn't mind being on the receiving end of that kind of affection every now and again. Even if it meant putting up with some teasing.

"You should have asked her."

Finn sighed. "Yeah. But then I was afraid she'd tell me."

Miguel got that. Man, did he get it. He'd been worried ever since learning Layla was going barhopping that she'd do exactly what she said she'd do. Find another guy and expand on that casual sex stuff she wanted so much.

Then he imagined what he'd do to any guy who touched her who wasn't him...or Finn.

"Didn't expect her to go out so soon after..." Miguel wasn't sure how to describe what the three of them had just shared. An affair? One-week stand? Relationship?

Finn didn't make him search too hard. "Yeah. Me either."

Both of them fell silent, letting the awkward moment stretch on too long.

"Listen," Finn said, at the same time, Miguel said, "Finn."

They both stopped talking, then laughed.

"You first," Finn offered.

Miguel shook his head. "You."

They were quiet again for a moment. And then they both started talking over each other again.

"We need LJ," Finn said, his words overlaying Miguel's, "Layla should be here."

Miguel sucked in a deep breath. "You want her with us?" he asked.

"Yeah. But I was afraid. I didn't want to...fuck, man. I didn't want to hurt your feelings, make you think what you and I could have wouldn't be enough. Maybe if LJ hadn't shown up when she did..."

"You're not hurting my feelings. I'm crazy about both of you."

Finn grinned widely. "Shit, yeah. I feel the same way. It's kind of fucking with my head a little. I mean...I love you, bro. I have for a while, even if I couldn't see it. Say it. Then LJ shows up and..."

"She's adorable. Funny. Perfect."

Finn nodded. "Perfect. For both of us. Just like we're perfect for each other. I've spent my whole life watching my uncles, seeing Sean and Chad together with Lauren, but I never thought...it never occurred to me that I might want the same thing. Oliver does. He says it all the time."

"It's different for him. Sean, Chad and Lauren are his parents. He was closer to it."

"Yeah, but Fergus grew up with my uncles Killian and Justin and Aunt Lily. And he didn't want it. Said he isn't wired that way."

Miguel considered that. "Not sure it's wiring. I think it's just three people who are lucky enough to find each other at the right time."

Finn thought about that, and when he looked back at Miguel, the smile on his face said he liked that idea. It was a brief response, then he sobered quickly. "Not sure LJ thinks this is the right time for her."

"Been thinking about that too," Miguel admitted. "I think it is. She just doesn't realize it."

Finn stood up and walked to the window of his bedroom, glancing out onto the side street. "Are you thinking what I'm thinking?" he asked, turning back to Miguel.

"We have to convince her."

Finn nodded. "With words or..."

Miguel laughed. "I say we seduce the hell out of her. Got my cuffs right here."

Finn came over and slapped him on the shoulder. "This is why we're best friends."

Miguel stood, ready to seal their newfound plan with a kiss, when Finn's iWatch pinged.

"Text?" Miguel asked, when Finn glanced at his wrist.

Finn shook his head as he tapped the face of the watch. "That's not the sound— Fuck!"

"What?"

Finn spun to his laptop, which was set up on the desk, and fired it up. "Padraig just pushed the panic button in the pub."

❦ 18 ❦

Layla walked into the pub and spotted Padraig alone, wiping up a table.

"We're closing," he said, before looking up and seeing her. "Hey, Layla. You're out late."

She nodded. "I was, um..." She glanced toward the doorway at the back of the pub, the one that led to the Collins Dorm.

Padraig grinned. "Darcy is up there if you wanna go visit. She's a night owl, so chances are good she's still up."

Layla considered going with that lie, pretending she was here to hang out with Darcy, but she caught the amusement in Padraig's eye. He knew why she was really here.

She glanced at the stairs and still hesitated.

"Something wrong?" Padraig asked.

"I can't decide if I'm about to make a huge mistake."

"You aren't."

"You don't even know what I'm talking about."

"Yes. I do. Be brave. Go upstairs, Layla."

There was something in Padraig's voice that told her he *did* understand, and it gave her courage. She took a deep breath and was about to walk upstairs when, behind her, the door to the pub opened. She wasn't paying attention to the door or Padraig. All that mattered was going upstairs.

When he shifted, his body language changing from relaxed amusement to aggressive tension, the hair on the back of her neck tingled.

"Layla, go upstairs," Padraig said slowly.

"No one moves," a creepy voice commanded.

Heart in her throat, she spun on her heel.

"Fuck," she whispered as Pennywise walked deeper into the pub, gun drawn.

He held up a bag. "Give me all the money in the register."

Padraig raised his hands. "I don't want any trouble here."

"Then fill the bag." Pennywise tossed it at Padraig.

Padraig grabbed the bag out of the air, using the movement as an excuse to step in front of Layla, putting his body between her and the gun.

Pennywise ducked his head, almost in a nod, then reached out and slapped the light switch. The main bar lights went out.

Layla sucked in a breath, frozen in the moment it took her eyes to adjust to the remaining ambient light from the beer signs on the walls and the small lights that illuminated the bottles behind the bar.

"I'm getting the money. Don't do anything." Padraig put one arm behind his back, motioning for her to flee out the rear as he started backing up so he could make his way around the bar to the register.

Layla took one step, but Pennywise took two jerky steps to the side, the gun rising higher. He was staring right at her.

Layla and Padraig both froze. Pennywise tipped his head to the side, staring at her even as he spoke to Padraig. "Don't try anything, or I fucking kill her."

"I'll fill the bag. Don't point the gun at her."

"Move faster," Pennywise said. It sounded like he was smiling behind the mask.

Padraig looked at her over his shoulder, then rushed around behind the bar, bag in hand.

"If you're fast...then I won't have time to do anything with her." Pennywise took one step deeper into the bar, the gun never wavering. His hand was steady as a rock. This guy wasn't afraid. If anything, it looked like he got off on this, enjoyed the rush of not just stealing from others, but scaring them.

Miguel had hypothesized the robber's motive was drug money. She wasn't sure she agreed with that right now. There was no desperation here.

Miguel also told her that during one of the latest robberies, the owner of the convenience store had managed to pull his own gun, but Pennywise had been quicker. He'd actually shot the gun out of the man's hand, like a sharpshooter in the Old West.

She backed up, her heart beating so hard that she could hear the *thump, thump, thump* in her ears, the sound nearly muting the ominous thud of his footsteps.

He took another step, and she retreated. As Padraig frantically shoved cash into the bag, Pennywise stalked her. She matched him step for step, backing up until her ass hit a table.

She didn't have a clue if Pennywise recognized her, the cheap mask concealing his features, every part of him from the shoulders up. She tried to recall Miguel's questions the first night they'd met, tried to find some sort of distinguishing feature that would help him crack this case. Pennywise seemed more at ease this time than he had the night he'd robbed her. She could only assume his success at evading the law so many times had inflated his confidence, made him cocky, but that detail wouldn't help Miguel.

He was close now, only five feet away. She couldn't retreat anymore, not unless she went around the table, and in the dim light, she wasn't sure she wouldn't trip over a chair. She'd had the sum total of one self-defense class with Finn and Miguel, and the number one thing they'd expressed was, don't be a hero. Miguel had reassured her that she'd done the right thing the first time she'd been robbed. She had remained calm and she'd given the man what he wanted. Just like Padraig was now.

Running and tripping over a chair was the opposite of being calm, but oh how she wanted to run, especially when Pennywise took another menacingly large, slow step toward her.

He was close enough that she could reach out and touch him. And he could touch *her*.

Layla closed her eyes for a moment, trying to keep herself calm. When she opened them, he was less than a foot from her, the grinning white clown face looming, filling her field of vision.

She started to scream, terror making her panic and forget to be calm, but Pennywise pressed the barrel of the gun against her lips. "Shhhh."

"Leave her alone," Padraig said, his voice still calm.

Pennywise leaned in, and as he did, he shifted into a dim shaft of light from a streetlamp outside. For a moment, his face was illuminated, and she could see his eyes, the only part of the man visible through the mask. And they were brown. Brown eyes.

Wow, that was really going to narrow it down for Miguel.

"What's taking so long?" Pennywise shifted the gun, running the side of the barrel along her cheek and then down her neck. With him this close, she could see his eyes moving, and it was almost more terrifying this way—the mask making his features fixed and still, with sunken, human eyes that moved and shifted in isolation.

It *was* taking Padraig a long time to fill the bag. Wasn't it? How much time had passed? Seconds or minutes? Was Padraig stalling? Waiting for something?

No one could see in, no one would notice what was happening. It was late on a Tuesday night. Sunday's Side, the adjoining restaurant, had closed two hours earlier, leaving that half of the building in total darkness.

Padraig had already pulled the blinds on the front windows before she'd gotten here, working his way through his closing routine. Miguel said the robber cased his businesses, knew the best time and way to hit, but if that was true, wouldn't Pennywise know there were a bunch of people living in the apartment upstairs?

She was starting to think this guy wasn't as clever as the police had thought. He'd simply been getting lucky.

"Here. It's here." Padraig remained behind the bar, holding out the bag of money. Layla understood his tactic. He was trying to draw the gunman away from her.

Pennywise grasped her upper arm roughly, jerking her in front of him. If seeing him had been horrifying, not being able to see him because he was behind her, the gun against the small of her back, his fingers digging into her arm, was far worse. He forced her to walk across the room toward Padraig. "Take the bag from him, coffee girl."

So he did recognize her.

God. If she'd thought herself terrorized before...now she felt practically catatonic with fear.

She took the bag from Padraig and tried to pass it back. He'd have to let go of her to take it.

Pennywise made a tsking sound, then started backing toward the exit. He was using her as a shield, keeping her between himself and Padraig.

"I gave you what you want. Leave the woman here."

Layla wasn't sure how Padraig had the ability to sound so freaking calm. She was so scared she felt nauseous. The urge to do something, maybe drop the bag and run, was strong. But there was literally a gun at her back. If it went off, she was dead.

Pennywise chuckled but didn't respond to Padraig. Just kept pulling her with him to the front.

He hadn't killed anyone before. He hadn't kidnapped anyone. Probably he was going to release her as soon as he was at the front door.

Probably.

Jesus. Please.

"I can feel your fear," Pennywise whispered.

Layla's eyes slid closed, and she knew that whatever this psycho had or had not done in the past, it didn't matter.

Tonight was different.

F INN FIRED UP HIS LAPTOP, CURSING WHEN IT TOOK THE screen too long to appear. As he typed in the password to the security system, he explained what he was doing to Miguel. "I installed the same security system here that I did at LJ's coffee shop. Finished the setup yesterday after..."

After Layla had walked away from them and Miguel had gone to work. He'd been too restless, too worked up to sit behind his desk at the office, so he'd come here instead and lost himself in the tech. He'd set up security cameras on the front and back doors—rather proud of how well both were hidden. Then he'd added three more inside the building, two in the pub and one on Sunday's Side.

Padraig had called it overkill, rolling his eyes at the panic button Finn had placed under the counter below the cash register. As he waited for the live video feed to fire up, he prayed Padraig had hit it by mistake. Even though he knew his cousin would never do that.

The panic button was tied to dispatch, just as any good alarm system was. So the Baltimore Police Department would have been alerted by now as well.

"Jesus," he whispered as the pub came into view. Padraig was behind the bar sliding money into a sack. Layla was standing backed up against a table.

And Pennywise was holding a gun against her cheek.

"Fuck!" Miguel turned and was halfway to the door before Finn caught him.

"We can't just run down there, Miguel. The guy has a gun on her."

"I'm going to kill that fucking clown." Miguel's gun was

strapped to a holster under his shirt. It always was. Baltimore cops followed a code—a cop was a cop twenty-four hours a day. Finn knew that well, having grown up with a cop dad. Miguel pulled it out, checked the safety.

"We need a plan," Finn said, everything he'd learned about security and diffusing hostile situations running through his head. "You know his MO better than anyone. What's he going to do?"

"Get the money fast."

"And his exit?"

"Always through the same door he entered. He'll already have scoped out the quickest, most discreet escape."

Finn went back to the video feed and reversed the cameras. "He came in through the front door."

"Cocky motherfucker," Miguel muttered.

"Come on. We'll go down the fire escape, circle the building, grab him when he comes out. That way, Padraig and Layla are out of the line of fire."

Miguel took off down the stairs. Finn stopped to grab something from the desk drawer, then followed, hot on his best friend's heels. Darcy, Gavin and Oliver looked surprised to see them running down the stairs like the place was on fire—and were even more shocked to see the gun in Miguel's hand. Finn tucked his hand behind his back, not wanting anyone to see that he was armed as well.

"Pub is being robbed. Lock the door and stay up here," Miguel said.

Oliver quickly went to the door at the top of the stairs and threw the dead bolt.

"Paddy," Darcy said, rising, her voice rife with concern.

"He's fine so far. Cops are on the way," Finn said. "Go upstairs, Darcy. Call dispatch and watch the live feed. Tell them everything you see."

Darcy raced up the stairs.

"What should we do?" Oliver asked.

Finn didn't want Oliver or Gavin anywhere near this. Though his youngest cousin was a man now, he was afraid he would forever think of him as his baby cousin, the tiny toddler who was always trying to keep up with the big kids.

"Ollie—" Finn started, prepared to tell him to lay low, even though he knew his cousin well enough to know he'd put up a fight and refuse.

"Watch the back from here." Miguel already had the back window of the apartment open, one foot on the fire escape. "If the guy tries to get away through the alley, watch him, chart his movements. Don't go down, don't follow him. He's armed and dangerous, so just watch. We need to know how he's getting away. It could help us catch him later if he eludes us again."

Oliver and Gavin nodded, taking up the sentry post at the window as he and Miguel quickly climbed down the fire escape.

"Finn," Miguel said, when they hit the ground. "Stay here and guard the back door."

Finn snorted. "No fucking way. You know he's not coming this way."

"You're unarmed. I can't take this guy down if I'm worried about you—"

Finn shook his head and started for the corner of the building. "Save your breath. There's no way I'm leaving you and Layla facing this guy alone." That was when Finn revealed his weapon. "And I'm not unarmed. Got my concealed-carry training from you, remember? License is upstairs."

Miguel cursed. "Jesus Christ. Don't fire that fucking gun. And stay behind me."

The two of them walked to the corner of the building, Miguel peering around toward the front door of the pub.

"What do you see?" Finn asked.

Sirens sounded in the distance.

"Fuck. That's going to spook—" Miguel stopped speaking— and that was when Finn heard the robber yell. His blood went cold.

. . .

THEY WERE NEARLY TO THE FRONT DOOR WHEN THE SOUND OF sirens cut through the night. They were loud and seemed to be getting louder.

"You called the fucking cops?!" Pennywise yelled.

Padraig's hands were in the air. "No. Of course not. How could I? Just take it easy, buddy. We live in Baltimore. There are sirens outside all the time."

Pennywise didn't calm down. If anything, he became more agitated. "Fuck!"

His grip on Layla's arm tightened, and she knew what he was going to do. Knew it because she felt the muzzle of the gun sliding up her back as he raised the weapon.

"Paddy! Get down!" she screamed as the gun came up, seemingly huge in her peripheral vision.

There was only a fraction of a second before Pennywise fired at the bar.

The sound of the shot was deafening, her right ear ringing and throbbing so painfully that for a moment, she thought her eardrum had burst. Padraig disappeared, but she had no idea if he'd jumped or if he'd been hit and fallen. She raised her right hand, slapping her palm over her ear as tears filled her eyes.

Pennywise used his grip on her left arm to shove her away from him. Disoriented, she spun, losing her footing. She crashed into a table with enough momentum that she and the table both went down.

She threw her hands out as she hit the ground, but she still banged her forehead on the floor hard. A second bolt of agony shot through her skull. Her ears were still ringing and for a moment, vertigo made her nauseous as the whole world spun drunkenly.

*Gun, gun, gun.*

Some still-functioning part of her brain was screaming at her. Her vision was black laces with specs of white. She had no idea where Pennywise was. Layla braced to feel the bullet, terrified that this time...fuck...this time he would shoot her.

She felt a whoosh of air as the front door opened.

He was leaving. Pennywise was leaving.

Her relief was short-lived when she heard Miguel yell, "Freeze!"

MIGUEL ROUNDED THE CORNER WHEN HE HEARD THE SHOT fired, so he was in close range when Pennywise backed out of the pub. He didn't let himself think about that gunshot or who the bullet might have hit.

He couldn't or he'd fucking lose it.

Pennywise jerked at the sound of his shout, turning to him, gun still drawn. Miguel had told Finn to stay where he was, safe behind the cover of the building, but he could hear him breathing heavily, knew he was right behind him.

It was strange how a split second could seem like hours. Between Pennywise shooting the gun in the pub to him standing on the street couldn't have taken more than five seconds.

And it was only a second more before the clown fired off a wild shot toward him. Miguel returned fire, and in the next second, Pennywise was flying back from the impact of Miguel's bullets, hitting the sidewalk hard, his body jerking just once before he stilled.

Miguel ran over to him, kicking Pennywise's gun from his hand even though it was safe to say the clown was incapacitated. He knelt next to him.

The whole thing couldn't have taken more than ten seconds. To Miguel, it felt like a lifetime.

Miguel had shot the assailant in the shoulder, shattered pieces of the man's collarbone poking through his skin. The other bullet had pierced his abdomen. The man was still breathing, though it was labored. And he was still conscious.

The sirens were louder now as one, two, three police cars

roared to a stop in front of the pub, officers emerging, weapons drawn.

Miguel put his hands in the air, aware that he was out of uniform. He didn't want any of his fellow officers to mistake who he was and what he'd just done.

"Put your guns down!" Aaron yelled, emerging from the third car. "It's Miguel."

Within seconds, Miguel was surrounded by police. Pennywise remained still on the pavement, not moving—he couldn't. He was losing a lot of blood.

Miguel reached up and pulled the mask off...to find a young Caucasian man, probably in his late twenties. His face was filled with pain. Miguel had never seen him before.

An ambulance arrived and EMTs moved in as Landon offered Miguel a hand, helping him stand.

Maybe a minute had passed. Maybe a bit more.

And that was when Miguel remembered.

Finn. Layla.

Both had been in the line of fire.

"Shit!" He spun around toward the pub, sucking in a huge gasp of air when he saw both of them standing in the doorway, looking at him. Finn had his arm around Layla. Miguel could see a bump on her forehead. Next to them—thank God—was Padraig.

Miguel smiled, exhaustedly taking a step, then another, toward them. They met him halfway, the three of them clinging to each other in a three-way hug as all their fears from the past half hour came out in a rush.

"When I heard that gun go off—" Miguel said.

"I heard you yell freeze and heard him shoot," Layla said.

"I thought you'd both be shot," Finn added.

None of them let go, the embrace going on long enough that Aaron stepped up to them, placing a hand on Miguel's shoulder to remind them they had an audience.

"You guys are going to have to let me in there to hug my

son," the older cop said. "Heard there was a shooting at Pat's Pub over the radio and had twelve heart attacks on the way here."

They broke apart with a laugh, as Aaron reached out and grabbed Finn into a tight fatherly hug. Aaron stepped back and studied his son's face. "You're okay?"

"Not a scratch on me, Dad."

"What the hell is that?" Aaron asked, glancing down to see the gun in Finn's hand. He turned to Miguel. "You armed him?"

"He armed himself, sir."

"Good. I'm glad." Aaron rubbed his jaw, clearly still pretty shaken up.

Miguel turned around to find Darcy, Gavin and Oliver all standing just inside the pub, none the worse for wear. Then his gaze shifted to Padraig. "Paddy? You okay?"

"Only injury sustained in the bar was the brand-new bottle of Crown Royal that got shot. Kinda pissed about that. Stuff's not cheap."

Aaron chuckled. "Call your dad. If Tris hears about this from anyone but you, he'll freak out. Where's Colm?"

"Date night," Darcy and Oliver said in unison.

"He'll be pissed he missed all the excitement," Padraig added.

"Jesus. I could do without excitement like this for the rest of my life," Miguel said.

Aaron looked over Miguel's shoulder at something, prompting Miguel to do the same. The EMTs were loading Pennywise into the ambulance.

"You caught him, son," Aaron said to Miguel.

"Yeah." Miguel had spent weeks trying to track down the asshole, so he should be celebrating. However, now that it was over, all he felt was...numb. It wasn't the first time he'd fired his gun in the line of duty, but it didn't make it any easier to see someone bleeding—bad guy or not—and know he'd been the one to cause that pain. "I should head to the precinct..." His words faded as he blew out a long, weary sigh.

"Paperwork will wait. I gave you another assignment for tonight. You follow through with that yet?" Aaron asked.

Miguel shook his head and grinned. "Only half of it. Then I got kinda distracted by a clown."

Aaron looked at Miguel, then Layla, then Finn.

Finn grinned when his dad studied his face intently. "I'm fine, Dad. I swear."

"Okay." Aaron glanced at Layla, who was far too pale. "You guys got everything in hand here?"

Miguel knew Aaron wasn't asking about the robbery. "Yes, sir."

Finn stepped closer to Layla, who was still visibly shaken, and put his arm around her, then he nodded. "Yeah. We got it, Dad."

"Captain Young," Higson called out. "You got a minute?"

Aaron waved to the young officer. "Call me in the morning, Finn."

"I will," Finn promised.

Aaron walked back to his vehicle as Miguel turned to Layla and Finn.

"My place?" he asked.

Layla pulled her keys from her purse. "We'll take my car."

Finn took the keys from her when they spotted her still-trembling hands. "I'll drive."

❦   19   ❦

"I think I lost ten years off my life," Finn admitted when they walked into Miguel's apartment. "Jesus. I can't stop hearing that gunshot inside the bar. Can't stop seeing that clown point the gun at you, Miguel."

None of them stopped at the front door. Instead, they kept walking, straight back to Miguel's bedroom.

Miguel scowled at Finn, even as he pulled off his shirt. "I told you to stay behind the building. You could have been shot, Finn."

Finn's eyes narrowed as he unbuttoned his jeans. "I'm always going to have your back, Miguel. You might as well get used to that."

Layla had been quiet on the ride from the pub to Miguel's apartment, and even now, she didn't join the conversation. Of course, she was sort of busy, frantically unbuttoning her blouse. Finn pushed her still-shaky hands away and took over for her.

"You okay?" he murmured as Miguel stepped behind her and unfastened her bra.

She nodded when the scrappy piece of lace hit the floor. "Ear's ringing. And I think I'm going to have a black eye tomorrow. But other than that," she said with a laugh, "I'm just peachy."

Finn gave her the laugh she seemed to need, but Miguel wasn't amused.

"We should have taken you to the hospital," Miguel said, even though he didn't stop shoving his jeans off, revealing his impressive erection.

"Not going anywhere." Layla reached out and gripped Miguel's cock, and Finn watched their cop's eyes drift closed.

What they were doing here was crazy. Nothing was settled between them, not even close. They hadn't said one word about Layla leaving, about their feelings for her, about what they wanted.

They'd all just stared down the barrel of a gun, and now...all he could think of was getting them naked.

Fuck it. He kicked off his shoes.

Crazy worked for him.

Layla looked over her shoulder at him, her gaze resting below his waist. She reached out with her free hand and ran her fingers over his crotch. The touch, even muted by the denim, hit him like an electric shock.

This wasn't going to last long for any of them. The adrenaline levels in this room were off the charts. Finn's dick was harder than it had ever been in his life.

"Get on the bed," Finn said as he stripped off his pants. "But wait." He halted Layla, peeling her sexy, tight jeans and panties off. Then he lifted her onto the bed.

After that, words weren't necessary.

Layla pushed Miguel to his back and knelt between his legs. She took his cock into her mouth, taking him deep on the first pass. Miguel's hands fisted in her hair, tugging it hard, the way she liked. The way that made her moan...like she was doing now.

Finn climbed onto the mattress and ran his hand over her upturned ass. God, she had the softest skin, the prettiest rear end. Before he could think about it, he lifted his hand and spanked it. He didn't hold back, so he knew from the sound, the way she jumped, the way it reddened instantly, it had stung.

Layla released Miguel's cock with a pop and looked over her shoulder at Finn. "Do that again."

Fuck. Yeah.

The burn triggered her arousal. Finn smacked her five more times on each ass cheek, holding back nothing, the stress, the relief, the fucking gratitude that they were all here, all alive, was flowing out in this no-holds-barred sex frenzy.

From the way Layla's head bobbed up and down on Miguel's dick, deep-throating him like her life depended on it, the way Miguel's grip on her hair was relentless, powerful, he knew they felt the same way.

They'd faced down death and lived.

Finn ran his fingers through her slit. She was soaking wet and so goddamn hot, he half expected to see steam rising from her pussy.

"Finn," she cried out, releasing Miguel's dick when Finn thrust three fingers inside her roughly. Her back arched and her legs parted, inviting—no, begging for—more. He thrust his fingers in harder, faster. Her orgasm struck fast, clenching his fingers so tight, he had to squeeze his eyes closed and count to twenty, lest he fucking come just from feeling her climax. It was insane. Neither lover had touched his dick yet, and regardless, he was right there on the razor's edge.

"Gotta fuck you, LJ. Jesus. Gotta fuck you hard," Finn said through gritted teeth. "Roll over."

Layla flipped to her back and Finn pressed her legs farther apart, his hips between her outstretched thighs. He'd double the foreplay next time. Right now, it was ride or die.

He slammed inside her as Layla's head reared back and she cried out loudly. Finn pumped hard, even as he reached for Miguel. "Straddle. Her. Head. Facing. Me." Every word was punctuated by another thrust.

Miguel shifted, his hiss sending Finn's gaze downward. Miguel's new position put his balls right above Layla's face and she'd taken advantage of that, sucking them into her mouth.

She'd wrapped one hand around the base of Miguel's cock and was pumping him with her fist, matching the rhythm of Finn pounding into her pussy.

Miguel leaned forward and kissed Finn. It was a hot, hungry kiss—all teeth and tongues—that ended when Miguel bit Finn's lower lip, drawing blood.

Finn wrapped his hand on top of Layla's, tightening their combined grips around Miguel's dick, even as he kept thrusting inside her. Harder and harder.

"Can't. Last. I..." Finn couldn't finish his warning. It was already too late. His balls constricted and he came, Layla hot on his heels. Her legs were wrapped tight around his waist and her body gyrated beneath him, climaxing hard.

Finn fell to her side, struggling to breathe. The air in the room was thick, humid. It was as if they'd traveled to the deepest, thickest part of the rain forest.

Miguel shifted when Layla reached out to him, and Finn realized his friend hadn't come.

"Shit, man," he murmured. "Sorry."

Miguel chuckled. "Greedy asshole."

Finn didn't bother to look guilty. He'd been called that before. On more than one occasion.

Miguel moved over Layla, caging her beneath him. "Brown Eyes, if you're sore or tired..."

"Come inside me," she whispered. "Please."

While Finn had pounded out the fears of the past hour inside her sweet, warm body, Miguel appeared to need a different kind of release.

His motions were slower, gentler. He stroked her body tenderly, looked at her in awe, and kissed her as if she was the most precious person on earth.

She was, Finn thought.

They both were.

They'd come to mean everything in the world to him, and he'd almost lost them tonight.

He watched for a few minutes more, then he twisted toward them, leaned closer until Miguel moved back so that Finn could kiss her. Then he kissed Miguel.

They lost themselves in those kisses, even as Miguel made love to Layla.

Love.

Colm was wrong.

This was no curse.

Miguel and Layla came together, their climaxes more peaceful, but no less powerful.

Miguel shifted to her opposite side, the two of them boxing her in between them. After everything that had happened tonight, after seeing Pennywise holding that gun to her cheek, Finn felt the overwhelming need to keep her with them, just like this, forever.

The three of them were quiet for a long time, but Finn knew they—like him—weren't sleeping.

Miguel was the first to break the silence, asking the same question rattling around in Finn's head.

"Why were you at the pub tonight, Layla?"

"I...I wanted to ask...for more time with you. Both of you."

Finn's heart stuttered, missing a beat or two as his eyes met Miguel's. He saw the same hope he felt reflected in his friend's gaze. Even so, Finn wanted—needed—clarification.

Because they weren't putting a time limit on this, and they weren't calling it casual anymore. Nothing about this was casual.

Finn rubbed his beard. "How much more time?"

Layla licked her lips nervously. "Well. Um...how about..."

"Consider your answer carefully, LJ. Say the wrong thing, and I'll whip your ass again until you admit the truth and tell us *exactly* what you want."

An adorable crease appeared in her forehead as she looked somewhat confused. "I swear to God, everything you say in the bedroom turns me on. I just got wet again. And I already had three orgasms."

"Miguel and I will take care of that wet issue in a minute. Tell us how long, LJ. How long do you want us?"

"Forever?" she asked nervously, lifting one shoulder as if she expected them to laugh or reject her offer.

Miguel did laugh, but not at her. Nope. There was no missing the pure joy in the sound.

"Hot damn," Finn said as he pulled her into his warm embrace. "You sure that's long enough?" he murmured in her ear.

She tried to pull back, to sneak a peek at his face to see if he was teasing her. Finn tightened his grip.

She glanced around at Miguel, needing to hear from him as well.

Miguel scooted closer, her back to his front, his lips at the back of her neck. "Forever sounds just fine. I'm in."

"So that's it?" Finn joked. "We're just hopping into a long-term, committed threesome with no discussion, no thinking?"

"You want to talk about it?" she asked.

He shook his head. "Nope. Nothing to think about. I'm in too."

# EPILOGUE

Finn snuck away from Miguel and Layla, who were sharing the couch with him at his parents' house. They'd all gathered together to celebrate Miguel's promotion on the force. The robber, Pennywise, had since recovered from the injuries he sustained and was currently in jail, awaiting his trial. He, Miguel, and Layla, along with Sunnie, Landon, Darcy, Pop Pop and Bubbles, had all gathered around the dining room table for a surf-and-turf feast.

After dinner, they'd decided to watch a movie. Pop Pop had declined, claiming he preferred to finish the current book he was reading. He said it was a mystery, but Finn and Mom had shared a knowing look and grinned. Pop Pop was a sucker for regency romances, a secret all of them knew, but didn't speak aloud.

"Be right back," he murmured, when Layla looked up at him questioningly.

Miguel nodded, whispering something to Layla. Most likely she hadn't heard what Finn had said. She was still suffering some hearing loss, the result of Pennywise firing the gun right next to her ear. The doctor said there was no way to know if it would be temporary or permanent—only time would tell.

She smiled at Finn, then turned her attention back to the

television while Finn traveled through the house until he reached Pop Pop's room. He knocked quietly, his suspicions about Pop Pop's reading material confirmed when his grandfather closed the book quickly and slid it under his pillow.

"Finn, my boy. Thought you were watching the movie."

Finn walked into the room, perching on the edge of Pop Pop's bed. "I've seen it before. Haven't had a chance to talk to you alone since…"

"Since your head started listening to your heart?"

Finn grinned. "Yeah. I wanted to thank you for opening my eyes to what should have been obvious."

"I knew you'd figure it out. You're a very wise man. Just like your namesake."

Finn shook his head. "I'm still pretty sure you're the Finn in that story. Not me. I've never been exceptionally knowledgeable. Solid C student, remember?"

"There are lots of different types of knowledge. Book smarts is just one. You're wise in other ways."

"Like?"

"Like how you treat others. You have an innate ability to find the good in everyone around you, you encourage others to be themselves. I don't think Miguel has had a lot of friends in his life. He and I talked about it once. He said he had a lot of trouble trusting people until he met you. With you, he felt free to be the truest version of himself. That's a very special thing, Finn."

Finn swallowed deeply, moved by Pop Pop's compliment. "Thanks," he said thickly.

"Come here. I want to show you something."

Pop Pop rose from the bed, jerking his head toward the wall of photographs that hung on what their grandfather called the "family wall." Each of Pop Pop's children and grandchildren had a frame, the pictures changing periodically, not due to the typical events of life, like graduations, birthdays and holidays, but rather, each photo seemed reflective of some simple, captured moment in time that spoke to Pop Pop's heart.

Finn's previous picture had been a much older one of him at twelve teaching Oliver how to ride a bike without the training wheels. Finn had always liked that photo, amused by the dirty knees of their jeans, their sweaty, red faces, the way they'd both been laughing. Pop Pop said that picture had perfectly captured Finn's personality, revealed so many facets of him. From the joy he took in life to the love he had for his family, from his sense of humor to his determination to teach Oliver how to ride that bike.

Pop Pop had changed many of the other photos on this wall, but Finn's had remained the same, year after year. Until now.

"Damn, Pop Pop," he breathed.

"Your dad snapped that last week, in the midst of moving day."

Finn remembered Dad taking it. Neither he, Layla nor Miguel had the ability to take things slowly as far as their relationship was concerned. Something had jarred loose in all of them after the night of the robbery at the pub, and they simply couldn't take each other, or life, for granted.

Once they'd committed to each other, there was no turning back, and on New Year's Eve, while tipsy as hell on champagne and shared kisses at midnight, Miguel—ever the instigator— declared it was time for the three of them to move in together.

As always, Finn and Layla had been all in.

So, they'd enlisted several of his cousins, his parents, and Landon to help them move. Layla's brothers, four scary, gigantic fucks who still weren't one hundred percent—shit, they weren't fifteen percent—on board with Layla's decision to engage in a threesome relationship, had helped as well. Though Finn suspected they'd offered their assistance merely so they'd have an entire day to flex their muscles and shoot intimidating looks at him and Miguel. Layla had rolled her eyes the entire time, chastising her big brothers, much to his and Miguel's amusement.

The photograph was of the three of them, resting on the stairs outside Miguel's apartment building. Layla was sitting on Finn's lap, leaning back against Miguel, who was behind her. Layla's arm was hanging loosely around Finn's neck. They were wiped out after a busy day of moving, but there was something about the way they sat, close, connected, completely at ease. Finn almost imagined he could touch the love flowing between them.

"All I've ever wanted for my kids, for my grandkids, is for them to find their person, the one who makes them better, makes them happy. You, with your big heart and big personality, found two."

"Pretty lucky, I guess," Finn said, grinning.

Pop Pop shook his head. "You'll never learn, will you? It wasn't luck. It was love."

Finn nodded his head toward where Pop Pop had tucked his novel under his pillow. "Good book?"

"Oh yes. Very good."

"Is the hero a duke or a pirate?"

Pop Pop chuckled and winked. "He's both. And the heroine is a bonny Irish lass."

"You ready to go home, Finn?" Layla asked. She and Miguel were standing in the doorway to Pop Pop's room. "The movie is over."

Miguel held up a plastic bag. "Your mom loaded us up with leftovers. Packed extra salmon for you since it's your favorite."

Miguel and Layla stared at them, confused by what was so funny, as he and Pop Pop laughed and laughed.

I HOPE YOU ENJOYED WILD SIDE. ARE YOU INTERESTED IN reading more about Layla's sexy Moretti brothers? Italian Stallions launches on January 25, 2022. First up - Tony Moretti in Down and Dirty. And yes...yes, it is a ménage!

HAVE YOU READ THE ENTIRE WILDER IRISH SERIES? ALL THE books are standalone, so they can be read in any order. Be sure to check out all of them!

Wild Passion
Wild Desire
Wild Devotion
Wild at Heart
Wild Temptation
Wild Kisses
Wild Fire
Wild Spirit
Wild Side
Wild Night
Wild Embrace
Wild Dreams
Wild Chance

TURN THE PAGE TO READ THE FIRST CHAPTER OF WILD NIGHT.

FANS OF WILD IRISH AND FACEBOOK! THERE'S A GROUP FOR you. Come join the Wild Irish Facebook group for sneak peaks, cover reveals, contests and more! Join now.

BE SURE TO JOIN MY NEWSLETTER FOR A FREE WILDER IRISH short story, One Wild Night.

# WILD NIGHT

Confirmed bachelor Colm is living the good life with a thriving law practice and all the freedom the playboy has come to enjoy. Until a city-wide blackout and the greatest sex he's ever had has him reconsidering his single status. Unfortunately, he doesn't realize the woman of his dreams is actually his lifelong frenemy, Kelli.

After a few too many drinks at a Halloween party, Kelli spends the night in the arms of a man who rocks her world. However, when she learns her mystery Mr. Right is Mr. Hell No, Colm Collins, she's ready to run for the hills.

But Colm refuses to accept just one wild night with her. He wants them all and the sexy man fights *dirty*.

Colm tossed back the rest of his Guinness, then glanced down toward the end of the bar at Pat's Pub. It was only Wednesday and he'd already had a bear of a week. As a lawyer who specialized in family law, he'd seen more than his fair share of contentious divorces, bitter custody battles, and tragic cases of domestic abuse. This week? He'd dealt with all three. Nasty shit. And it felt like it was ripping out chunks of his soul.

Typically, he could keep emotions out of it, could focus on

the task at hand. If it had just been one case, he could have held it together. But he was dealing with three. The three worst cases of his career. All at the same time.

He caught Padraig's eye and pointed to his empty mug. His twin narrowed his eyes briefly, but Padraig knew him well enough that he didn't question him. Instead, he just picked up the empty mug, pulled the tap, refilled his glass, and then set it back down in front of him.

"Wanna talk about it?" Padraig asked.

Colm shook his head. "Nope. Just want to forget about it."

"Yeah, the fact you're on your third beer in less than an hour...on a weeknight...sort of clued me in. You sure you—"

"I'm sure," Colm interjected.

"Okay. Well, I'm here if you change your mind."

Colm managed a weak smile and a nod. He knew that, knew his brother would always listen to his troubles, would have his back in a fight, would give him shit whenever he did something stupid. They were brothers and that was what they did. Add in the whole twin-bond factor, and it was safe to say no one on the planet got him like Padraig.

He took another sip of his Guinness, leaning back in the stool, savoring the quiet white noise of the pub. This place, this very stool at the bar, was probably one of his happiest places on the planet. So as soon as he'd dragged his sorry ass in from work, he'd plopped down with no more thought than he was home and beer was close.

He loosened his necktie and unbuttoned the top button of his shirt, releasing a long sigh.

He could have walked right by the bar and headed upstairs to the apartment he shared with some of his cousins. After all, it was empty right now. Darcy had gotten a new job recently and had been putting in long hours, excited to prove herself as a graphic artist, while his other roomies, Oliver and Gavin, were working late at a construction site with Uncle Killian and Uncle Justin.

Colm would have had the entire apartment to himself, something that was rare, given the number of family members who treated the place—the Collins Dorm—as home base for...well... practically everything. Pretty much every Collins celebration took place either here in the pub or upstairs. From graduation parties to bridal showers, his huge, crazy, fun family always managed to find something to celebrate, and damn if they didn't do it in style.

Just this morning, Darcy was buzzing around the apartment, her excitement almost tangible as she pointed out that with their annual Halloween party happening this weekend, they were kicking off the official "Collins social season." After the Halloween party—which Sunnie and Darcy had been planning for ages—it was one festivity after another as they hosted Friendsgiving, Thanksgiving dinner, a Christmas party, and then rang in the New Year in serious style.

Colm was exhausted just thinking about it. Which was unusual for him. He always looked forward to family events, but this year...this year it felt like hard work.

Shit. The job really was getting to him.

He rubbed his eyes, then kept them closed, breathing in and out slowly. He'd almost found peace when there was a loud scratching sound of the stool next to him, sliding across the floor.

"Fucking fuck of a fucked-up day."

Colm sighed. He should have gone upstairs.

He didn't bother to open his eyes to acknowledge the new arrival. "Hey, Kell."

"What the fuck is wrong with you?"

He glanced over and saw her looking at him curiously.

"Were you asleep?" she asked.

He shook his head. "No. I was relaxing. And it was working. Until you showed up."

Kelli rolled her eyes, completely unrepentant about disturbing him. Not that he should be surprised. They knew each other far too well for her to ever genuinely take offense over anything he said. Same went for him.

Kelli had been Padraig's best friend since kindergarten. Leave it to his twin brother to pick a girl as his best friend. And not just a girl but Padraig's polar opposite. Padraig was an easy-going, quiet, gentle soul.

Kelli, on the other hand, was brash, loud, opinionated. She and Colm had butted heads for as many years as she and Padraig had been friends. Probably because, as Colm's mother liked to point out whenever he bitched about her, she and Colm were too much alike. Which Mom insisted was probably the reason why Padraig adored Kelli so. As if that was supposed to make him like her better.

"Hey, Paddy," Kelli called out when Padraig returned from the stockroom with a new bag of peanuts. "I need a glass of cab sav. A *big* glass."

"The nine-ounce pour?" Padraig teased.

"You stop at nine ounces and I'm going to kick your ass. Actually, save the glass. I'll just drink straight from the bottle."

Padraig laughed as he placed the wineglass in front of her, pouring red wine all the way to the rim.

Kelli lifted it gingerly, careful not to spill a single drop as she took a big sip, then sighed dramatically. "God, Paddy. You're the greatest man I've ever known."

Padraig rolled his eyes, then put the bottle of wine in front of her. "Just in case I'm not here the second you drain that first glass."

"Marry me," she said, the joke a standard. Kelli had asked Padraig to marry her no less than seventeen million times over the years.

And Padraig always gave her the same response. "You're too much woman for me, Kell. It just wouldn't work."

"Speaking of marriage...where's Emmy?" Kelli asked, wiggling her eyebrows playfully at Padraig.

Only Kelli could get away with such a segue.

Over the course of the past year or so, Emmy Martin had become a regular at Pat's Pub, the quiet romance author achieving what only one other patron in the history of the business had managed. Her own saved spot at the bar. Padraig had placed a permanent reserved sign at the end of the counter for her since it was the place Emmy set up camp almost daily as she wrote her books.

The only other person with a saved stool was Pop Pop, though his was front and center, as the fun-loving man needed to be right in the thick of "the action" at the pub. Colm had figured out a long time ago that "action" meant Pop Pop had the seat with the best view of the big screen TV that hung behind the bar to watch whatever sport was in season, and a prime location for hearing any and all of the gossip shared.

Padraig pretended to be annoyed by the question. "Ha ha, Kell. Emmy is not here tonight."

Kelli had been trying to convince Padraig to ask Emmy out for months, but his twin wasn't budging.

Padraig had been married once to Mia, the love of his life. She had been everything to him. So even now, two years after her death, his brother was still struggling to put the pieces of his life back together.

Lately, Colm and Kelli had found one thing they actually agreed on, and that was that Padraig needed to move on with his life. He'd been hiding behind the counter of this pub for far too long.

Plus, as more time passed, it was pretty obvious Emmy had the hots for Padraig. And while he was resistant to romance, he and Emmy had formed a pretty solid friendship.

"Where is she?" Kelli pressed. "Emmy's always here. She's the reason I stopped by. I wanted to talk to her."

"She has a nasty head cold. I'm running some of Aunt Riley's chicken noodle soup over to her after my shift ends." Padraig looked at his watch. "Which is in about ten minutes."

"Taking her soup, huh?" Kelli asked. The woman was relentless when it came to Padraig and Emmy.

"As friends, Kell. I always bring you chicken noodle soup when you're sick too," Padraig pointed out.

"Yeah. Shit. You do. Come here. Lean closer."

Padraig sighed heavily, even as he did as she asked, perfectly aware of why Kelli had made the request.

She lifted her hand and stroked the side of his face. "I just can't get used to you without the beard."

Colm and Padraig had sported beards since the year they'd turned nineteen, placing a bet on who could grow one the fastest. Colm had won, something he still gave Padraig shit about, but even after the contest ended, neither of them shaved.

Then, out of the blue last week, Padraig had shown up at the pub clean-shaven, simply telling everyone who asked why that he'd just needed a change.

Colm wondered if it wasn't something more, but no amount of questioning on his part—and he was a lawyer who knew how to get the goods from a witness—had produced a different response.

"How many times are you going to touch my face?" Padraig asked, though he didn't sound as annoyed as he pretended.

"It's just so strange."

"Good strange or bad strange?" Padraig asked.

Kelli considered that. "Good strange. Truth is...you look super hot like this."

"Please," Colm said, jumping into the conversation. "He has a baby face. You won't catch me shaving *my* beard off. Don't want to look like some wet-behind-the-ears teenage boy."

"You're just jealous because you couldn't pull off the look," Kelli said, jumping in, as always, to defend Padraig. It was another standard operating procedure. Kelli always—as in one hundred percent of the time—took Padraig's side in any argument with Colm, no matter what.

"That makes no sense," Colm said. "We're twins, Kelli. Identical. Twins."

"You know, I always forget that," she joked. "It probably has something to do with the shape of your mouth. The way it's always open and producing that annoying sound. Distracts me from all your other features."

Colm grinned and doubled-down. He'd had the day from hell, and the idea of blowing off some of that steam by engaging in a battle of put-downs with Kelli sounded pretty good to him. "The only annoying sound I hear right now is—"

"Oh, look at that," Padraig said, glancing at his phone. "My shift just ended."

While Colm and Kelli loved to trash talk, it drove Padraig up the wall. His brother really was too freaking nice sometimes.

Colm watched as Padraig's replacement, one of the new part-time bartenders, stepped through the hinged opening. His brother filled the new guy in on who was drinking what, and then said goodbye to them, heading back to the kitchen, no doubt to grab the soup for Emmy.

He and Kelli both took another sip of their drinks, neither of them bothering to pick up their previous conversation, and as the silence stretched, it occurred to Colm that the two of them were rarely alone together.

Kelli took another sip and, for the first time since she'd sat down, he noticed the dark circles under her eyes. She also hadn't changed out of her work attire before coming here, and he was amused by her orange sweater that featured a glittery black cat in bunny ears. She had a wide array of ridiculous clothing like that. He knew none of it fit her tastes, and that she wore it just because her kindergartners loved it.

She was taller than most women he knew, just an inch or so shy of six feet tall. Sometimes he wondered if that was why she'd continued to hang out with Padraig throughout school. He and his twin, at six foot four, were in the minority when it came to guys taller than her.

Her dark auburn hair had gotten longer in the last year. All through high school and their twenties, she'd kept it shorter, the thick, wavy mass barely touching her shoulders. He wasn't sure what had prompted her to grow it out, but he had to admit—begrudgingly—it was very pretty on her. He liked long hair on women, gave him something to hold on to when he was...

Fuck.

He turned away from Kelli, unwilling to finish that thought.

For a hot minute, he'd had an image of taking her from behind, his fist gripping that long hair.

Jesus. Maybe he should lay off the Guinness.

Kelli sighed, capturing his attention again.

*Oh, to fuck with it.* She didn't annoy him so much that he couldn't admit she was actually very attractive. She had one of those unforgettable faces with high cheekbones, porcelain skin, full, red lips, and an ever-present twinkle in her eye that some might mistake for humor, but he recognized as mischief.

When she'd first gotten boobs in sixth grade—*big* boobs, the kind that captured a young boy's attention—Colm had fancied himself interested in her...for about three seconds.

Unfortunately, that was the same year his dad had thought he and Padraig should sport crewcuts, for some insane reason. His interest in Kelli ended the second she'd dubbed him "Chrome Dome Colm," the nickname sticking for the better part of the school year, before he'd put his foot down with his dad that summer and insisted on growing his hair out again.

After that, his crush on her had ended, and their rivalry had elevated from hair pulling and rude nicknames—she'd been Smelly Kelli most of first grade, thanks to him—to eye rolling, smirks, and practical jokes.

"So you had a bad day too?" he said.

She nodded once, then shrugged. "Lately, it's felt like one long string of bad days. But yeah, today was especially shitty."

When it became obvious she wasn't going to go into any details, he prodded. "What happened today?"

She glanced at him suspiciously, and he understood why. The two of them weren't small-talk friends. Actually, Kelli liked to refer to him as her best frenemy, something he hadn't bothered to deny since the term fit. If they were talking, they were bickering.

"My cat got sick in the middle of my new rug first thing this morning. I didn't see it, so I stepped in it, barefoot, and slipped. I hit the edge of the coffee table, so I now have a bruise on my hip the size of Kansas. Then I was running late to work, rushing around my place like a lunatic, looking for my goddamn keys, and I spilled coffee all over my outfit."

"That sweater wasn't your first choice?" Colm didn't bother to hide his grin.

Kelli didn't take him to task for it. Instead, she gave him a weary smile back. "All of that happened before eight a.m. Work wasn't much better. My hip hurt like a bitch. Believe me. Five-year-olds have sonar when it comes to sore spots. I swear every single one of the little rascals managed to bump into that exact spot today. Then one of my kids shit his pants—the smell was ungodly. After school, I had to sit through an eternal faculty meeting where we learned about a new round of budget cuts that basically ensure I'm going to continue to spend half my paycheck on supplies for my classroom."

"Damn."

"Yeah," she said, lifting her wineglass and draining it.

Colm reached over and poured her a new glass from the bottle Padraig had left in front of her.

"Thanks. So...that's why I'm willing to face tomorrow with a hangover. What number Guinness are you on?"

Colm drained his beer. "That was three." He lifted a finger and the part-time bartender came over and refilled it.

"Damn. Four beers," she murmured. "Wanna talk about it?"

Padraig had asked the same question, and he'd turned his brother down. For some reason, maybe given the fact she was in the same funk and the beer was starting to work its way through him, he didn't mind sharing with her.

"I'm working on a few rough cases. The worst of which is a contentious divorce with a custody battle that's going to guarantee the kids are in therapy for the rest of their lives."

Kelli frowned. "Young kids?"

For her tough exterior, Kelli was pure marshmallow inside when it came to children.

"Four and six."

"Fuck. Some people really shouldn't be allowed to have children. All they do is fuck them up."

"Yeah. Tell me about it. I'm also representing a woman in the middle of a domestic violence case, and I'm pretty sure she's going to drop the charges and go back with the man who put her in the hospital not once, not twice, but four times."

Kelli sighed. "Jesus. I don't know how you do that job."

Colm gave her a crooked grin. "Hey, at least I don't have to clean up shitty underwear."

Kelli tapped her wineglass against Colm's mug. "Good point. So...are we going to be the voice of reason for each other at the end of these drinks, or are we going to take this to the next level?"

The question was pure Kelli. He knew if he paid his tab and said good night, she'd follow suit. They'd both head home, pass out, and while they'd have headaches in the morning, they wouldn't be too much the worse for wear.

But if he ordered another beer, she'd finish the bottle of wine —and maybe even order another—and they'd both pay dearly at work tomorrow.

For Colm, there was only one answer. "Next level."

She grinned and took another sip. "Game on."

They continued to bitch about their days until her bottle of wine was drained and he'd finished beers number five and six. After that, they moved on to tequila, though at least they'd been somewhat intelligent and ordered food as well. They complained about their jobs until the bartender yelled out "last call."

"What time is it?" she asked.

Colm glanced at his phone. "Almost midnight."

"Damn. Made a critical error. Came to the wrong Collins twin for moral support. Paddy would have switched me to coffee after glass number two and poured me into a cab."

Colm shrugged unapologetically. "Hey, you gave me a choice."

"Yeah, I did." She glanced toward the door. "I guess I should..."

"Did you drive here?"

She nodded. "Really only intended to have one glass of wine while I chewed Paddy's ear off."

"Come upstairs. You can sleep in Finn's room. Sheets are clean. Set your alarm early enough that you can go home, shower, and suffer through a hungover Thursday."

Kelli stood up. "That sounds perfect. I don't feel like being alone tonight."

Colm felt the exact same way.

Read Wild Night now.

# ABOUT THE AUTHOR

Virginia native Mari Carr is a New York Times and USA TODAY bestseller of contemporary romance novels. With over two million copies of her books sold, Mari was the winner of the Romance Writers of America's Passionate Plume award for her novella, Erotic Research. She has over a hundred published works, including her popular Wild Irish and Compass books, along with the Trinity Masters/Masters Admiralty series she writes with Lila Dubois.

*Find Mari Carr on the web at*
www.maricarr.com
mari@maricarr.com